THE SECRET INSIDE BERRYHILL MOUNTAIN

BY SUE CORY PERSON

outskirtspress
DENVER, COLORADO

This is a work of fiction. The events and characters described herein are imaginary and are not intended to refer to specific places or living persons. The opinions expressed in this manuscript are solely the opinions of the author and do not represent the opinions or thoughts of the publisher. The author has represented and warranted full ownership and/or legal right to publish all the materials in this book.

The Secret Inside Berryhill Mountain
All Rights Reserved.
Copyright © 2016 Sue Cory Person
v2.0

Cover image courtesy of Betibup33 Design. All rights reserved - used with permission.

This book may not be reproduced, transmitted, or stored in whole or in part by any means, including graphic, electronic, or mechanical without the express written consent of the publisher except in the case of brief quotations embodied in critical articles and reviews.

Outskirts Press, Inc.
http://www.outskirtspress.com

ISBN: 978-1-4787-7891-2

Outskirts Press and the "OP" logo are trademarks belonging to Outskirts Press, Inc.

PRINTED IN THE UNITED STATES OF AMERICA

Chapter One
Rude Awakening

THE SOUND OF a scream hurled me three feet past the end of my bed.

Scampering to pull up my over-sized pajama bottoms, I scurried across the floor toward Cassandra's bed. The wooden floor in our large second story room was always cold, and certain patches were worn down to abrasive. I flinched as a splinter sliced through my fingers. The darkness of the room disoriented me, but I knew her bed was close. I crawled on my hands and knees until I touched something solid—the metal desk. Cassandra's bed was beside it.

I prayed she was in her bed before I swiped my fingers across bare sheets. A sliver of light caught my attention as it appeared abruptly, slicing a line across our vast room. The light funneled up from the staircase. My insides clenched as another high-pitched scream tore through the empty silence. There was no mistaking the familiar voice. It was my older sister, Cassandra.

I pressed down my fear and dashed from the room toward the stairs. The stairwell light was on as I approached, but it took a moment for my brain to register what I was seeing. I gasped at the sight of my mother huddled like a frightened girl at the bottom of the stairs. My sister Cassandra was standing one step above her screaming at Tab, my stepfather.

An uncontrollable urge to vomit overwhelmed me and it flew against the paneled sidewall, then dribbled down the stairs, narrowly missing Cassandra's white tennis shoes.

"Momma!" I bellowed, moving forward.

My mother's head jerked to look at me, her expression changed from distraught, to aggressive as quick as a flipped light switch. She spoke sternly, "Joey! Stay upstairs!"

Cassandra glanced my way without a break in her shrill vocal. As I took a step back I recognized her plan, a strategy of distraction.

I pulled my hurt feelings together and followed her lead. I began yelling "Tab, please stop! Please don't hurt Momma!" It all seemed surreal and I could barely hear my own voice.

Mom sat crouched on the bottom step, shielding her head as my stepfather loomed over her, swaying his arms back and forth. I was thankful each time—his long arms missed. The sound of his voice had always stirred my insides, it was loud and condescending. But today it was laced with foul, perverse cuss words.

Mom's body language was submissive, she was not fighting back. I heard words come from my mouth, although they were faint, "Mom come upstairs." I wished with all my heart she would get up and run upstairs.

Cassandra stood firmly planted above Mom, with her hands balled into fists and her face red from screaming. When she realized her screaming was having no effect, she turned and ran up the stairs. Her face was etched with fear as she squeezed past me.

I felt bad. She saw this coming, and had shared her feelings with me last night. I wished I had taken her seriously. But my imagination just hadn't gone to the place hers had when she'd whispered her fears into my ear. She had a strong premonition that things would accelerate to this point. Mom had sent us upstairs ten minutes earlier, and I was comfortably settled into my separated space. I was wrapped up tightly in my blankets, ready to assume my standard sleeping position facing the wall, when Cassandra's warm breath penetrated my ear. Her fingers latched onto my chin, and with a vigorous tug, she pulled my face toward her and looked me in the eyes.

"Joey, sleep lightly. I have a very bad feeling that something bad is gonna happen."

I examined her distorted face, confused about what she was talking about. "Because Tab's not home yet?" She quickly nodded, then climbed into her bed, fully dressed. That should have been a clue. She has never, as long as I can remember, ever gone to bed dressed. I'd ignored her warnings in favor of the peaceful serenity I was feeling. After all, Mom and Tab hadn't had a fight in weeks, and the last few fights hadn't reached a "call the police" state. Sure, Tab was late, which had been the source of my happy mood. I had no intentions of sleeping lightly but told her I would, as I snuggled back into my sleeping position. The fact that she'd made an effort to be taken seriously—crawling over to my bed, staring into my eyes with such intensity—should have made a stronger statement. I carried the guilt with much regret wondering if this night could have been averted.

Tab's voice jolted my eyes back to Mom "I'm not through with you woman!" Mom had tried to get up and he pushed her back down. She covered her head as he pushed her face down to her knees.

Cassandra had reached the south window, facing our neighbors and started a new level of high-pitched screaming. We didn't have a home phone, but most of our neighbor's did.

Jody and Jessica, my nine-year-old twin sisters, had awakened. A new surge went through me when I saw they were coming to see what was going on, I looked down the stairs and saw Mom still under Tab's broad swings. Without giving myself time to think or Mom time to stop me--I jumped forward and ran full force down the stairs. I dove over Mom and into Tab's chest knocking him backward, away from Mom. Tab crashed to the floor and his head slid into the wall with me still on top of him. I looked into his face ready for his anger to be directed at me, but his eyes were shut and he mumbled something incoherent. I climbed off and he made no effort to retaliate or get up.

The twins helped Mom get up and over to a kitchen chair beside the stairwell.

My heart was out of control as I opened the front door while keeping my eye on Tab. I wasn't sure what I would do if he tried to get up, the thought of Mom's cast iron skillet went through my head. I heard Mom's voice and stretched to listen. Jody turned and spoke softly to me, "Go see if anyone heard Cassandra."

I looked at Tab and his eyes were still shut, he had not

THE SECRET INSIDE BERRYHILL MOUNTAIN

moved. I hoped he had passed out from drunkenness. I ran up the stairs to Cassandra and her head and shoulders were stretched outside the window, and her backside and legs dangled on the inside. She was speaking to someone below.

We lived on a street that had an alley between our house and the house next door. Our neighbors, the Lawson's, had heard Cassandra's screams and were gathered below the window, staring up at us in concern.

Cassandra sighed with relief as she turned speaking to me, "Mr. Lawson's calling the police." I looked down and saw Mr. Lawson running down the alleyway toward his house in a slow but rhythmic pace, his checkered housecoat barely covering his large body. I rushed back to tell Mom and the twins, and within minutes we heard sirens in the distance. We hadn't told our neighbors what was happening, but it wasn't the first time we'd asked for help, so I was sure they knew.

The police arrived and jostled Tab till he groggily opened his eyes. I heard the handcuffs lock onto his wrists and his voice trying to sound reasonable, "I wasn't gonna hurt her, I just needed to teach her a lesson. You've been there before, haven't you buddy?"

I prayed they wouldn't fall for his acting and felt relieved when I heard the officer answer, "You're the one that needs to be taught a lesson . . . buddy."

The medics tended to Mom. We stayed in the stairwell watching the goings-on. One of the officers noticed the four of us and came over. He looked tall in his perfectly pressed grey uniform and as he removed his hat, he ran his hand through his thinning, blonde hair, as if he was readying himself for the job at hand. His voice spoke softly and his eyes filled with compassion as he corralled us to the top of the stairs. "Let's wait upstairs while the paramedics tend to your mom. That is your mother, isn't it?"

"Yes," the four of us replied in unison, nodding our heads.

As a rule, we were shy around strangers, especially the twins, who are the youngest at nine and two years younger than me. Cassandra was twelve and one year older than me, I turned eleven last summer. Even though I didn't have a shy bone in my body, Tab's low tolerance for talking, had all of us, what he called . . . "well trained." He himself bragged to others, "Joey talked like a motorboat when I first married Marleen. That was before I told him to 'Shut-up! Kids are to be seen and not heard!' Now we don't hear a peep out of him!"

"Well, I'm Officer Matt Darden, but you can call me Matt. Do you kids have anyone we could call, maybe a grandma or aunt?" He focused in on Cassandra, most likely because she was the oldest and looked it, she was tall for her age and her thick dark hair was cut short making her look like a teenager.

"Not really," she stammered, and before she could say another word, Jody, the most vocal of the twins, had her hands cupped around the officer's ear.

"He drinks too much beer," Jody whispered. Officer Darden took on a serious nature, then looked at Jody, asking for her name.

"That's Jody!" I blurted.

"Jody . . ." Officer Darden's voice was easy-going and regulated. "I appreciate you bringing that information to my attention. I'll write that in my report." He took out a notepad and scribbled a few words. "I know this kind of thing happens sometimes."

Cassandra started to cry, which shocked all of us; she very rarely took a break from her in-control-of-every-situation attitude. "It's not sometimes at our house," she exclaimed, "more like every night."

Officer Darden stopped writing and looked at Cassandra. "You mean this kind of thing happens every night?"

Jody leaned forward and spoke in her usual, informative nature. "He doesn't knock her around every time. Sometimes he just yells." Jody then leaned back, looking satisfied she was able to straighten out the facts.

Jessica, the more reserved twin, touched the officer's arm to get his attention. "We like it best when he doesn't come home at all."

She was right about that, the only fun we had in life was when Tab was gone. He demanded "quiet" every moment he was home. We would sit at the table with homework or reading, then would move to the couch or front porch and wait for bedtime. I can remember tip-toeing to the bathroom only to jump at his yell, "Who's stomping through the house!"

Mom sat with us; when Tab didn't make her scratch his back. Which was several times a week.

"Well look at the good side," Mom would say. "All four of my beautiful children have excellent grades because of all the quiet study time!"

I grumbled at the memories, then spoke to officer Darden, "He's not our real dad. Our dad lives in Texas. His name is the same as mine, Joseph Oren Cory, but you can call me Joey." I extended my hand to Officer Darden feeling a little bit like a fake, I didn't really know much about my dad, I was turning three when Mom took us to California. It's been an off-limits subject for as long as I can remember. All I know about my dad is his full name and what Cassandra had told me. "He was nice, and he would set me up on the grocery counter and give me candy." I wish I could remember that and him.

"I'm very glad to meet you, Joey." The officer shook my hand, then scanned our faces. "You're the most polite children I've ever met."

An officer dressed identical to officer Darden looked up the stairs, "She's asking to see the kids."

Officer Darden's face softened as he spoke, "Go on down."

We went down the stairs and huddled around Mom, all four of us crying. She was in a tall rolling ambulance bed, centered in the living room. Mom hugged each of us, then told us to sit on the couch. Officer Darden pushed the rolling bed close to us, but was looking and speaking to Mom, "I don't know if you . . ."

Mom butted in, "Oh I do . . ." She twisted a pale cotton coverlet between her fingers, "I was too embarrassed about all this to speak, but I recognized you right away."

"No need for that," He said.

I could see for a moment her thoughts drifted away from the problems at hand. Her expression lightened a little as she looked his way speaking, "You've been a regular at Warren's Cafeteria for quite a while now. It's Officer Darden isn't it?"

"Yea . . ." He half smiled.

I knew this chopped up conversation must be referring to

Mom's work. She began working at Warren's Cafeteria, even before we moved here. She held the record, for working with no missed days. Not one day absent in one year and eight months work.

Officer Darden pointed to us as he whispered, "You spend some time with the kids and I'll be in a chair close by."

Mom turned her attention to us, reaching her hand forward to wipe a tear from Jessica's face. "I'm okay, Jess."

"You may be okay now, Mom, but what about next time?" Jessica's stress was evident in her tone.

Without hesitating, Mom spoke firmly, "There won't be a next time, Jessie. This was the last time he will ever lay a hand on me. I promise."

I had to admit, Mom sounded like she meant it.

An officer came through the door and we could see Tab in the backseat of the police car, he began yelling to Mom, "Marleen! Come get me out!" When the screen door slammed shut, Mom flinched.

Officer Darden stood up when Mom flinched. "Mrs. Randal can I speak with you, alone?" Mom directed us to move to the end of the couch so they could talk. Officer Darden sat down in front of her.

"Call me, Marleen," she mumbled through her swollen lips.

"Marleen," Officer Darden said, "I don't know the whole situation, but the Sergeant told me you're not pressing charges, if that's the case you need to take the kids and go stay with a relative. Find somewhere safe until he calms down. Twelve hours is all they will hold him, unless . . . I can convince you to press charges?"

"I can't do that," Mom barely uttered as she looked down at her chest.

A sadness melted across the officer's face. "The laws are plain—we won't force you, but I strongly suggest you leave. Get out of here and start a new life. At the very least, stay gone till he gets some help."

"We don't have anywhere to go." Cassandra spoke after eavesdropping, but her words were true. Her face was still red and swollen from her earlier bout of hysterical crying. She looked worn out, and listening to her words was heart wrenching. I looked at the twins who were agreeing with Cassandra.

Officer Darden sat silent for a moment before speaking, "If I find you a place, will you go?"

Mom hesitated till she heard Cassandra's voice, "Mom. . ."

"We will go." Mom said.

He went out to the porch and spoke with his Sergeant. I kept him in view, and he talked for a long time. He came back and pulled his chair up to Mom. He leaned in and they whispered back and forth, till he stood up, "I will be here tomorrow morning. You and the kids get a good night's sleep." A visible sense of relief washed across all four of us, still sitting side-by-side on the couch. We had no idea what he had in mind, but it brought new feelings of hope, knowing he was going to help us.

We listened as the paramedic tried to talk Mom into going to the hospital, but she wouldn't even consider it. I knew why: there was nowhere for us kids to go. The paramedics moved Mom to her bed, doing all they could under the circumstances.

Officer Darden handed Mom his card. "You call this number if you feel you need medical attention and I'll get the medics back out here immediately." Mom thanked him repeatedly.

A serene look encompassed her face as she readjusted herself in the bed; she wasn't accustomed to being pampered. Cassandra plumped up Mom's pillow, pushing her fist in both ends. The twins snuggled up close, one on each side. I positioned my head on the pillow next to Jody, and after realizing it smelled of my stepfather's Aqua Velvet cologne, I pushed it to the floor. Fighting back the tears, I covered my face. I sure wished we could push him out of our lives as easily as I had pushed his pillow to the floor.

Chapter Two
Thoughts of Joy

NOISES FROM MY stomach woke me up. I guess after losing my dinner down the stairs, my stomach was pretty empty. It was still dark, but the nightlight glowed from the nightstand to the ceiling and back down across the bed. To the average person it would look as though we had the remnants of a late-night slumber party. Not so. In fact, the girls and I have never been allowed to have a sleep-over. Tab didn't allow things like that in the "Randal" house. His opinions and lectures on life were long and depressing, most of them left me wondering if he was ever a kid himself--because fun was not allowed in his world. His favorite beginning line, besides "kids are to be seen and not heard" was, "This generation of young vipers are ruined rotten!" And I knew the story by heart that followed, "When I was your age I worked pulling cotton till my fingers bled. Ten hours a day with only one noon meal, and half the time my meal was gone before I got to it!" We had never met his parents and from his stories of childhood I was glad. My real dad hadn't been down to see us at all (at least not that I know of). Cassandra made excuses that he didn't know where we lived. But I later found out he mailed letters; because I saw the remains after Tab burn them. I had made up my mind then and there that I would have nothing more to do with my stepdad other than being respectful.

I navigated my way up and over to exit the bed. I didn't want to awaken anyone, especially the twins, because I was pretty sure there wasn't enough cereal for three.

Crossing through the living room I turned on a lamp. The living room was in mass disorder. No doubt the residuals of Mom's struggle. I hadn't noticed it in the chaos of last night. Mom's book collection was strewn across the floor and it made me mad. I picked up the leather binding of "The Wizard of Oz" from the center of the room, it was separated from its pages. "Alice in Wonderland" was on the top of a heap that had been pulled from a fancy wooden shelf Mom displayed them on, away from our reach. She cherished her Book Club editions and told us, it was the only thing of value she took when she left our dad. I gathered them up, so upset, I lost my fight against new tears. I understood what Mom must have went through before we awoke to help her.

It was a terrible night, but I had hopes for better. And the book collection going back together with no permanent damage was proof. I set the shelf on the floor and put the books back in the numbered order, believing our lives could be put back together too. The plan could work as long as Mom's words were true, that my stepdad would never lay a hand on her again. The only spoiler I could see, was Mom's soft heart. Numerous times after fights, Tab would cry his way back into her good graces, promising it would never happen again.

Our duplex was located close to downtown and that's why we rented it. Mom's work. She worked downtown and she could walk from home. The kitchen was small and narrow, and more like an afterthought than a real kitchen, with barely enough room to walk through. The living room was strange in that it had doors on all sides, with a door leading to the one bedroom downstairs, which was Mom and Tab's room. A door to the kitchen, a door to outside and a door to go up the staircase. The only bathroom was upstairs, but the main upstairs room was as big as the downstairs. The twins shared a big full-sized bed, Cassandra and I each had a single bed.

The other side of the duplex was a mirror image of our home. Not sure why, but the other side remained vacant. We'd been here for over a year and not a soul had even looked at it. The front porch was one long cement slab, stretching the full length across both units and cement stairs went down all three sides. A small roof, covered each front door. The door to the other unit had never been locked even though it was full of old but nice-looking furniture. Someone had covered everything with white sheets and left.

I quietly rummaged through the kitchen, looking for the box of cereal I had hidden the morning before. My assessments were correct; crumbs flowed from the box after my bowl was full. I wiped up my mess after adding milk, then crept outside to the porch with my supersized bowl of Fruity Pebbles.

The neighborhood was populated with mostly older people. A few were friendly but most stayed to themselves.

Out of habit, I checked the driveway across the street and replayed the memory of one of the best days of my life.

I had been sitting in this very spot when a boy named "Roy" came with his father to visit the older man who lived there. He was only nine, but we had three hours of pure pleasure. We played tag, hide and seek, chased each other around our duplex, and then we sat on the porch and shared a root beer he'd procured from the elderly man's ice-box. Kindred spirits from the get-go. I was so sad when his dad came out and told him to get in the car, that it was time to go. I sat silent as I watched him cross the street, then stood up and yelled before he got in the car, "Will you be back?" I had hoped with every fiber of my being that he would say yes, but he shrugged his shoulders, and climbed in. The wood-paneled station wagon drove away and his smiling face peered through the rear window, never to return again.

As I slurped down the last bit of multicolored milk, I heard a car turn down our street. I jumped to my feet, fearing it might be Tab. My instincts always instructed me to stay out of Tab's way. I ran for the door, where Mom appeared, fully dressed. Before I could get a word out, she said, "Pack your clothes, Joey. Officer Darden is here."

"Good morning!" came from behind me. I turned around and saw Officer Darden walking toward us. He looked different this morning, he was still in uniform, but his face had a suntanned glow, showcasing his blue eyes and large dimples.

"Go pack a small bag, Joey," Mom repeated. She touched my shoulder as I walked through the open door, "And Joey, thank you for putting my book collection back together." I smiled--pleased she had noticed.

All of my clothes could fit into one bag, so I found a grocery sack and pushed everything I owned from my designated bottom drawer into it. The girls were fighting over who was gonna take the one hairbrush we all shared. Cassandra stomped over and threw the hairbrush into my bag. "Let Joey take it. Mom says we don't need to take anything. He might need it, where-ever he ends up going!"

Now that didn't sound good! So I spoke up, "Am I going somewhere different than you guys?"

Jody imploded from the bathroom. "Joey, it's only temporary!"

I changed my tone from mad to whiny. "That's not fair. I wanna go with you guys."

Mom came up the stairs with Officer Darden following close behind. I could see she was emotional. "Joey . . ." She spoke in a subdued manner. I dropped my bag of clothes and prepared for the worst. "Officer Darden found us a place to hide from Tab for a while." Her large brown eyes instantly filled with tears while I looked on. She closed them tightly as if she thought she could hide from the disappointment on my face. My eyes never left her face as she sniffled and pulled a chair to set in front of me. All was silent as she took the tissues Cassandra was offering. I waited as she blew her red, chapped nose, dabbing carefully around the swelling. "This is short-term," she whispered softly to offer me a thread of hope. "Just until Tab has time to cool off."

"Why can't I go?" I wiped my wet face almost as quickly as my words came out. My three sisters inched closer, and I took a tissue from Cassandra. Mom wrapped her arms tightly around me, too emotional to speak. I felt safe and warm, and for a moment I thought I had won, that I would be going with them. Her hand affectionately circled my back, then she lifted me away with a pleading look on her face, asking me with her eyes to please be understanding about this.

"Honey, I hate this more than you can ever imagine." Her voice cracked. "Officer Darden secured us a spot in a private shelter for women, and no men are allowed." She took a deep breath before continuing, "Joey . . . He spoke with Mr. and Mrs. Lawson and told them our situation and they would love for you to stay with them, just for a bit."

"But, Mom, I'm not a man, I bet they let boys in . . ." I crossed my arms, pouting. "I don't want to stay with Mr. Lawson, I wanna go with you."

Pausing, she looked at me with her worn-out eyes. She was silent for a moment before she softly said, "I know, sweetie."

Officer Darden came over and sat beside us. "Joey, I tried so hard to get them to let you come, but they threatened to not let any of you come. Son, your mom needs a safe place and enough time away from your stepdad to get her life together."

I knew he was right, and in the back of my mind I knew if Mom was still here at the duplex when Tab came home, she would take him back . . . she always did. Mom sat me down beside her. Her chin quivered as tears rolled down her cheeks.

No one talked. No one knew what else could be said to make me feel better.

After a long gap of silence, Officer Darden spoke up, "I knew this would be the most difficult part, and if it proves to be too much . . ." All eyes were on him as he stopped speaking in the middle of a thought. His eyes thinned as if his ears strained to hear his brain. After a moment his facial structure relaxed, and a new gleam was in his eye. An idea had just formed in his head and we watched it happen. He looked at me intently. I wondered if maybe, he thought I heard it too. I shook my head in a dumbfounded way.

"Marleen," he said, "can we talk?"

The two stood just inside the bathroom, talking with hushed voices. The metal bathroom thresh-hold stayed in my view, as I watched for their feet to exit. I was anxious. I couldn't imagine not living with my mother or sisters, even for a day. A feeling of dread washed over me because it was taking so long. I prayed under my breath he had come up with a brilliant idea, because I knew, if not, in the end, I would have to do it, stay with the Lawson's so Mom could go start a new life without Tab.

Mom's black flats stepped over the thresh-hold. She had a pink ribbon in her hand and asked where the brush was.

"Inside my sack." I pointed to my bag of clothes. In one quick movement, Mom had the brush in hand and pulled it through my thick black hair. Dark hair and dark eyes reflected back through the mirror. Not just me, but Mom and Cassandra and Jody and Jessica. I looked up and Officer Darden's blonde hair and blue eyes looked out of place. Our lineage was half-Choctaw and half-Irish, but with my shoulder-length black hair, my distinct appearance screamed Native American. Mom was 100% Choctaw and her great grandfather was a Choctaw Chief. I was proud of my ancestral heritage, and Mom battled Tab on many occasions to let me keep my hair. I hadn't had a true haircut since I was five years old. Mom placed a pink hair ribbon around the ponytail she had combed tightly, halfway up the back of my head. The girls were squatting down at eye level, looking me over.

Laughter erupted when Cassandra said very seriously, "With your thick eyelashes Joey, you make a very pretty girl." I smirked ready to release sarcasm, but thought better of displaying any dislike to what might be the only option I had available. I smiled and batted my thick eyelashes.

"Let's see what you think," Mom said as she pointed me toward Officer Darden. His brow furrowed.

"I know this was my idea, but I really don't know." He pinched his chin as he was thinking. "He looks great and would most likely pass as a girl." We all waited for the "but," and then it came. "But . . . do we want Joey to have this memory? I'm no psychologist, but I would hate to be the one to scar him emotionally, by forcing him to live a period of his life as a girl." He sighed. "Also, I've never been on the inside of the women's home, but from what I hear it's so spectacular that no one ever wants to leave."

Mom looked slightly taken aback. "Oh my goodness . . . no. We will only be there long enough for Tab to quit looking for me. Three months at the most."

That was encouraging enough, so I spoke up. "You're not forcing me! I can deal with being a girl for three months, Mom, if it means I can stay with you." My eyes told her that it was the only plan I could deal with.

Chapter Three

Road Trip to a New Life

OFFICER DARDEN DROVE us in his personal car and our first stop was under the big red "Warren's Cafeteria" sign. Mom was smiling when she got back in the car. "I have a job waiting for me, after I get things in order." She held up a check, "and three months paid leave." Matt started to clap and we joined in. A small celebration that embarrassed Mom, but she began clapping.

"It's a three-hour drive," Matt stated. "Have you kids heard of that big hillside amusement park?" We all shook our heads. "It's a multimillion-dollar complex built into the side of Berryhill Mountain. Rollercoasters of every size!" My insides quivered with excitement at the word "rollercoaster." I looked over at my sisters, who joined me giggling with sheer delight at the thought of such a place.

"Mr. Berryhill has a huge clothing line and invests a lot of the profit back into the park," Officer Darden lowered his voice and whispered, "He also funds the Berryhill Women and Girls' Rescue Community." We all raised our eyebrows in admiration.

"He must be a very rich man!" Cassandra exclaimed.

"Oh, he is. He is known all over the world for his philanthropy, and he gives away more than most people make. But what some may not know is that he also owns the world's biggest and best amusement parks. His largest park is in Japan, his home country, but Russia and the UK have a close second. Nine in all, spread out across the globe. Now, whether or not they have the women's homes, I couldn't tell you. This one is strictly confidential. The only reason I know." He stopped midsentence and was silent for a moment. I figured it was deeply private information and he was trying to decide if he could trust us with it. I looked up just as his voice spoke five very subdued words. "The only reason I know . . ." He forcefully finished with an obvious push. "My mom lives there."

I immediately looked at Mom and her reaction, she did a double take at his confession; which told me she didn't know this before he said it. I bet she was looking at this whole thing a little differently now, I was.

Matt seemed almost relieved he was able to tell someone the secret he had been holding inside. He took big breaths then continued. "My sister and her boyfriend were trapped in the drug world. She lost custody of their baby, but wouldn't abide by the judgement, she hired people to steal the baby back. Mom and my niece have been living in the home to protect my niece for eight years now. I haven't heard from Mom, but that is standard procedure for their safety. I truly believe things are good for them, and I can be happy, knowing they are happy."

"What's her name? I can give her a message for you?"

Mom exuded compassion.

Matt's dimples and smiling blue eyes looked at Mom, then back to the road thinking. "Thank you Marleen. Her friends call her Ruthie, but her real name is Ruth Anne Darden. As far as what to say, you can just tell her all is well with me and I love and miss them both." This was the first time any of us had seen behind the curtain of his personal life. It was pretty clear he missed his mom. Mom enthusiastically agreed she would relay his message and Matt gently closed the curtain and focused on telling us fun facts about Mr. Berryhill's amusement park. A new spirit filled his words. My sisters and I watched his animated face in the rearview mirror, as he told us more about the park. "The amusement park is five miles long and five miles wide. Sixteen thousand acres of pure amusement. I don't know how large the women's compound is, but when you see the park and the grand way Mr. Berryhill builds, one has to believe it's every bit as impressive." We all agreed.

Two hours went by quickly, and my Fruity Pebbles had long since worn off, I tapped Mom's shoulder and whined under my breath to the back of her ear, "I'm getting hungry."

"No worries, Joey, I got that taken care of." Officer Darden turned his head to look at me. "I know a little hamburger place that's right around this next corner." A few seconds later, he pointed ahead to the right. The side street was marked with a hand-painted sign that read, "Claude's Hamburger's." We turned down a long gravel road that was lined on both sides with tall, slender pine trees. Between each tree was a whitewashed sign with lively green cursive that read, "Welcome to Claude's!" "You are here!" "Best burgers in town!" "Best food around!" A small house sat at the end of the road, painted the same green color as the cursive on the signs, and a circular gravel driveway wrapped around the front. Parking was in the grass, and quite a few cars filled the yard.

"It doesn't look like much, but don't let that fool you. These are the best patty melt sandwiches you will ever eat!" Officer Darden said.

I was excited even though I had no clue what a patty melt sandwich was. Officer Darden parked the car and we all piled out. The air smelled of fried food and yummy goodness. We sat around a big round table and Mom gave Officer Darden full control of ordering for all of us. We shared three patty-melt combo meals. The waitress arrived with three large serving plates overflowing with a mound of cheese-drizzled fries and grilled sandwiches. The sandwiches were cut and Swiss cheese oozed down the inside, bubbling down from the meat onto the buttery toasted bread. We each ate half a patty melt with fries and washed it down with a chocolate shake. We weren't accustomed to eating out, and I had never had my own chocolate shake before. Mom passed around the napkins as the conversation turned serious. Officer Darden proceeded with all the rules and regulation's he stated as mandatory, and then added, "must be followed to the letter." He made a point to look at each one of us individually. "Agreed?" We nodded our heads in agreement.

"No phones or contact with anyone outside of the compound. The safety of a lot of women would be at stake if that rule was broken. You will be assigned a home and you are responsible to keep it clean. The kids will attend a year-round school and uniforms will be supplied."

I snarled at the thought of year-round school, but the visual in my head of wearing a girl's uniform scared me. Suddenly realizing, being a female twenty-four hours a day and seven days a week could be complicated, I became nervous because this "pretending to be a girl" thing really was going to happen. I suppose since no boys are allowed; they only have girl's bathroom's and showers; and if someone saw me undressed it could be disastrous. At the very least, I would be ridiculed and at the very worst—Mom would be kicked out. My mind took inventory of all the little things that might draw suspicion, like I have big feet, my legs are bruised and my knees are huge and boney. When I pictured them in a uniform dress, "Argh!"

Matt snapped his fingers, "Are you listening Joey?" I jerked my head up from thought and he continued. "They will assign you a job, Marleen." He spoke in a personal tone, as he looked at Mom. "I'm sure they will let you fully recover first, but if not...you speak up." The rules and regulations seemed to be endless, and I wondered how in the world Matt could remember all that stuff.

As we got back into the car, we waved good-bye to the isolated little hamburger joint that we knew we wouldn't see for at least three months.

The ride was peaceful. My three sisters had dozed off, and Mom and Matt were talking. I heard him ask her how she'd met Tab. I listened closely, because I had never heard Mom talk about it.

"Joe and I were married thirteen years and we were doing well. We owned a big ranch out in the country, a grocery store in Dallas. He was great with the kids and he knew how to have fun. We went to the drive-in movie every Friday night, but then something changed. He changed. He would leave the store early every morning and wouldn't get home until almost midnight. One day he came home and told me he had met someone and they were in love. He packed a suitcase and left. The next day he hired an expensive lawyer and filed for divorce. The judge surprised us all when he made Joe sell everything, giving me and the kids half the money."

Mom stopped talking for a moment and just stared out over the vast countryside. She cleared her throat before she continued. "I had never been alone before. Joe and I got married when I was just fourteen, so I had no worldly experience. My only thoughts were that I wanted to get out of Dallas. I bought a new car, loaded up the kids, and went to California—that's where my mother was at the time. A few months later I met Tab and fell for all of his lines. We got married in a year, and then it took another year for him to go through all that money. We moved back to Oklahoma broke. Tab and my mother never got along, but she passed away a little over a year ago and she was the last of my family."

I could tell it made Mom sad to talk about her life. It made me kind of sad too. Matt looked at Mom closely before speaking, "I know how hard all this is Marleen, but you taking control of your life is a good thing. For a while you may be out of your comfort zone, but keep pushing through, there will be light at the end. You've taken the first step toward a better life for you and your kids." Mom had started to cry, but smiled at his words.

The rest of the ride was quiet and I fell asleep. The car coming to a stop woke me. I sat up as we pulled off the road onto the grass.

"I need to go into detail about how this is gonna go down before we get inside Berryhill Park," Matt said as he pointed to a picnic table within walking distance. "Let's use this table." He stood tall at the end of the table and asked which of us had the best memory. Cassandra raised her hand.

"She is gifted in that area," Mom agreed.

Matt spoke slow and deliberate as if our lives depended on us executing every detail properly. "First," he said as he looked me over, "we need to decide a name to call Joey that everyone can remember."

Cassandra raised her hand. "What about a name close to 'Joey'; that way if we slip, we can say we call her 'Joey' for short."

"That's a great idea!" Mom said, and Matt agreed.

"What about 'Joy'?" Jody contributed with enthusiasm.

"That's good." Matt pronounced it several times. "J-o-y—that almost sounds the same." He looked at me, raising his eyebrows questioningly to make sure I was okay with it.

"That's good," I said. "It does kind of sound like 'Joey' if you say it slow." With claps of approval, I raised my hand and officially announced my new name, "Joy."

Matt pulled out a small map of the park that showed every square inch, including the mountain's skeleton that encompassed the whole five mile west side. "There are four rollercoasters, but only one starts on the northwest base of that mountain. This is the only way in to the hidden home." He turned the map, showing Cassandra the other three rollercoasters on the other three sides of the park. She looked at it closely, then closed her eyes to seal it in her memory.

THE SECRET INSIDE BERRYHILL MOUNTAIN

"This rollercoaster is called Silver Lining Express, but some know it as the Old Forty-Niner. It has forty-nine cars. Each car holds six people. There are five of you, so make sure no one sits in that extra seat." He glanced at each of us to be sure we understood. "You will be in the last car. This car is only added when there is a delivery to be made to the compound. Halfway through the ride, it will pass the west corridor for the second time. A hidden wall will move and your car will disconnect from the rest, allowing it to go straight. It will follow the track past the wall and take you inside the compound. Make sure your lap-bar is tight; it may cause quite a jerk."

"Will you be with us?" Jessica said, looking a little scared.

"No. I show my badge to get you into the park. That's as far as I've ever been allowed."

Jessica and Jody looked at Mom, who was trying to reassure them. "Don't you worry, girls, Officer Darden wouldn't send us if it wasn't safe."

Cassandra stood up. "When you consider the alternative—being at home when Tab gets there—this will be a piece of cake." We all laughed; Cassandra could always point out the positives. Cassandra was wise beyond her years and being the oldest, the blow of all this drama affected her the most. She wasn't afraid of Tab, like I was. Many times Cassandra took on the role of arbitrator during Tab's out of control rants. And ... If he was sober enough to hear her, he would back down. I remember at one point Tab crying and even saying he was sorry for his temper. It was during one of those times when he talked of his childhood, I could see he was repeating the cycle of abuse he and his mother went through.

Matt looked down at his watch. "By my calculations, Tab is getting a ride back to the duplex as we speak."

Mom's face went solemn as she spoke, "Sure glad we won't be there."

Matt tugged on my ponytail as we walked back to his car. "You will have a little time to enjoy the park before the four o'clock rollercoaster departure."

"That will be awesome!" I said with a smile. I slowed down to walk beside him, thinking to myself, *I sure wish Mom had married someone like him.*

Chapter Four
City on the Hill

"ONLY A FEW minutes away," Matt chided, cultivating our nervousness. He readjusted his sitting position, straighter and taller to get a good view. "Get ready to keep your eyes on the sky. Right when we come up from the valley, to a brief hilltop, we'll get a spectacular overall view of the park." All four of us moved forward, with our hands clinching the back of the seat. "Now!" he yelled.

I could see it off in the distance! The car filled with verbal acclamation. We crept slowly along, enjoying the beauty of it. A masterpiece collection of castles and amusement rides, sitting on the side of the mountain, with Ferris wheels and Merry-go-rounds prominent throughout. And the ultimate treat: it looked as though a big rollercoaster encircled the whole enchanted community. Finally, my eyes came to a stop on the backdrop of the massive mountain range; the purple glow from low-hanging clouds was just spectacular. I had never seen anything like it before. And to think we lived relatively close made it even more incredible. We all sat back in our seats, excitedly talking about how big and magical this place looked to be.

The traffic started backing up a few blocks out and Matt kept looking at his watch. "We may have to park farther out than I wanted and take the tram up to the gate."

"That's fine," Mom said, looking at all of us as she spoke.

Matt pulled down a row marked "ZZ," then followed a light green tram that was half filled with people. An officer wearing an orange vest pointed us to an open parking spot. We quickly got out and ran to the waiting tram. We sat waiting as passengers loaded on, my anxious insides gurgled. I looked down to calm my stomach, hoping to quell my uncertainties but jerked my head back up after seeing my short, stubby toes in pink flip-flops (an extra pair the twins had found for me). This whole being-a-girl thing was going to take some getting used to. Mom looked over her shoulder at me and crinkled her brow.

"I saw my fat feet in the flip-flops." I groaned. She smiled at me. She was beautiful, inside and out. Mom's father died before I was born, but she told me once she had her father's big, dark, almond shaped eyes and high cheekbones. I think about that every time I look at her. Mom had a sweet, innocent nature about her and was kind to a fault; I'd never heard her say a harsh word to or about anyone. I was sure that was why she'd stayed with Tab, even though we knew she was miserable. The thought of her having a better life made this easier, and a boldness rose up inside me, fueling me. *I can do this!* I thought proudly.

The tram inched its way up to the gates and some passengers moved to unload. Matt sat motionless. We followed Mom's lead and stayed in the tram as Matt flashed his badge to another officer across the walkway close to the gate. Matt then pointed to us and nodded his head. I looked at the other officer, who also held up his hand and nodded his head. It sure looked like a secret signal. After a moment, the tram came to a stop and we unloaded. We waved good-bye to Matt and I felt a little sad. I enjoyed spending the day with him and hated to have it end. After crossing to the sidewalk, Cassandra ran back and gave Matt a hug; we all promptly followed. I realized a few things that day: Not all men were like Tab, and we had met a new friend who truly cared about us.

The park officer's stern, ill-disposed look, told me he didn't encompass the same radiant qualities as Matt. He handed us a new map and cautioned us not to be late. "You only get one shot at this," he snarled, walking off.

Mom made a sour face at his departure. She looked at her watch. "We have a little over two hours. Let's go find the west-side rollercoaster first, and then we can relax." The mountain range was west, so we followed the lane marked "Golden Gate West."

Jessica, who was studying the map, assessed her findings. "It's marked 'Golden Gate East' on the opposite side. It's obvious whoever named the walkways knew it might be easy to get lost." We soon learned the walkways were named after bridges across the country.

Everything seemed to be sprinkled with happiness. Brightly colored musical rides lined the five-mile stretch, with miniature castle structures housing restaurants and game rooms. One tall castle had a staircase wrapping around the outside edge, encircling it to the top. At the very top, which was several stories high, you could board a slide that ended up somewhere down the lane, but I couldn't see an end. The sections I could see were lined with small hills, bumps, and curves to enhance the ride along the way.

I looked at Mom and pleaded with my eyes (the draw of that ride had slapped me across the very fibers of my being). She stopped the girls to look at her watch again. After a small pause, she said, "Let's give it a try!" She was jubilant, echoing the words she knew I was dying to hear.

The girls jumped with pleasure as I wrapped my arms around Mom, squeezing tight. "Thank you, Mom!"

The line of people waiting to ride this one was short. Mom thought it was because of the treacherous climb up the spiral staircase that circled steeply around the tall castle structure. I pumped my legs like a machine, never stopping once. My legs were shaking from muscle fatigue by the time I made it to the top. The ride attendant watched me climb, he said I made it to the top in record time. After Mom crested the top, we were handed a feed-sack mat and given instructions to stay on it as much as possible, because the ride down could cause skin burns. The slide was long and yellow and exciting. I pointed out to the others, "Look, it ends up at the base of the mountain. This will take us to the Silver Lining Express!" The slide had five lanes across, so we waited until we could ride down together. Watching all the fun of those going before us--made me giddy.

The teenage ride operator joined in the fun. "One and a half miles of open air roller coaster! Hang onto your hat and try your best to stay upright! The highly polished polyurethane will give you the ride of your life!" When he saw we were all going down together he held up his arm and spoke in a challenging goad, "When I count to three, jump on your mat and go. And may the best man win!" He circled his arm like he was winding up the motor of our anticipation, "One! Two! Three!" He yelled the numbers enticingly slow, then in a baritone voice, "Go!"

All five of us pushed off with our hands and flew down the slide. I quickly picked up speed with the starting hill's immediate steep decline, it dropped almost straight down. The rush of air almost choked me, but I felt free and alive as I zoomed down the slide, my sisters and mom were screaming with glee behind me. The sun reflected onto the gleaming yellow slide, glowing with the appearance of being freshly waxed, which would explain the silky, smooth glide. Floating over the first big hump made me feel as if I was flying. I closed my eyes as the wind blistered through my face and pushed on my shoulders. When I opened my eyes, I laughed hysterically as the transitory lift had propelled me a foot in the air. This was so much fun! I found myself drooling (no doubt from the continual smiling). It seemed to go on forever, up and down, in and out, dips and curves bouncing us all around. I could hear Mom on the next slip, laughing like a young girl. Cassandra was to her right and squealing in delight. I heard the announcer come on the intercom and scold the twins; they were breaking rule number three: "no holding hands." The twins made it to the bottom first, dancing around in victory. I was pleased with second place. Cassandra came in third and had a frown on her face as she slid to the bottom. The twins ran to help her up.

"Now this is having fun!" The twins giggled. We were having fun at a whole new level, the most fun I'd ever had.

Mom had no problem with being last; I wondered if she'd planned it that way.

"That was exciting!" Mom proclaimed, still laughing as she slid past the end, landing next to a pair of painted bins. She jumped to her feet, instructing all of us to put our feed sacks into the yellow containers marked, "Return Mats Here!" We sat down on the spectator bench to recover from our splurge of fun and watched as others swooshed down giggling with joy. Mom stood in line to get us a soft drink and came back with four red-and-blue snow cones. It was a beautiful day and a day we would remember.

Jody pointed across the walkway. "Well, there it is." It was the entrance to the rollercoaster we were scheduled to board. A line stretched down the Golden Gate Walkway. The sign above the opening read, "Berryhill's Silver Lining Express." Reality faced us head-on. We sat silent, finishing our two shared soft drinks.

"Let's go," Mom said, jumping to her feet. We ran to the end of the line, fearing we might have waited a little too long, because the line was growing rapidly.

"There are forty-nine cars, Mom," Cassandra reminded, as she started counting people. "At six per car—"

"Two hundred and eighty-eight!" I blurted.

Suddenly, a shrill whistle filled the air coming from the loading port. The officer from the front gate dropped his chain-clad whistle and gestured for us to come forward. Mom worked us through the crowd and up the stairs past the officer's scowling face to the last car. Apparently, he was waiting for us to board first. As soon as we sat down, the chained restraint was dropped, allowing the line to move forward. People rushed to fill the seats, a furious surge to get the best seat for the four-o'clock departure of the Silver Lining Express.

Chapter Five
Rollercoaster to Paradise

THE SIGN READ, "Enter at your own risk—thirty minutes of non-stop excitement!"

"Thirty minutes..." Mom groaned.

"Now that's my kind of ride!" I answered.

No one was allowed in the car to the front of us, and we soon learned why. The uniformed officer checked our safety bars then climbed into it. I sat back in my seat, anxious for this to get started while butterflies filled my stomach. I wondered if all this sitting was included in the thirty-minute ride time. It was taking forever for the attendant to get everyone seated and buckled in.

Mom and Cassandra were in the front two seats of our car, and Jody and Jessica sat behind them. I sat in a seat by myself and leaned back as I admired the mural on the curved wall. The colorful painting followed the wall around, then extended into the dark tunnel we would soon enter. Larger than life was a scene of threadbare people walking past an old locomotive, toward a brightly illuminated city perched on the top of a distant hill. It seemed obvious to me that someone intended a story in this picture. The abandoned train was meticulously painted in great artistic detail, even down to a family of birds nestled inside a loose metal fitting. It gave the impression that this train had been the essence of luxury travel in days past but now sat broken. The large group of people had no intentions of fixing it or waiting for it to be fixed. They had made up their minds to walk to that prosperous, glowing city. I yelled up to Cassandra and Mom and asked what they thought about it.

After marveling over the artistic skill and beautiful use of color, Mom said, "I think that's called an allegory. A picture with hidden meaning." Mom studied it to see what the painter was saying, then spoke, "Don't let a problem stop you from getting to that greater place." The twins liked that.

Cassandra stared at the painting and then lifted her face as if she were at a recital, speaking to a crowd. "Maybe it's a correlation to life and that big, shining city is heaven. You know, for those who are suffering. It seems to say, 'Life is hard and full of problems, but don't stop. Heaven is to be our ultimate destination.'" As usual, she elaborated more. "No earthly vessel can get you there. You just have to walk it out on our own!" Looking pretty proud of herself—she had always been the smartest girl in her class—she smiled profusely as she stared at the painting.

"That's quite good," an attendant who had been listening interjected. "Actually, Mr. Berryhill wanted it to be his creation, up on the hill, and people are coming to his world to find happiness." Everyone close enough to hear, started clapping, responding with words of praise. Obviously, the amusement park was a place of joy for a lot of people, and those people loved Mr. Berryhill for providing it.

I felt movement as a voice came over the intercom and said, "Get ready for the ride of your life!" The announcer had a rhythm and zing to his voice.

I hung onto the bar in front of me and kept my eye on the officer to see if he did the same. He turned to Mom and nodded. "Good luck to you and your family, ma'am."

Mom smiled and patted him on the shoulder. "Thank you," she said.

I examined the wall, while we rolled into the dark tunnel, looking for any sign of an opening that we would later enter. The mural must had been hiding a trap doorway. Bam! With a sudden thud, it felt as if someone had dropped us onto an underground high-speed rail line. All forty-nine cars went from zero to fifty in a split second. It was totally black and the screaming was amplified inside the mountain. I heard Mom yelling for the girls not to worry. "Just close your eyes and hang on!"

My stomach felt like it was riding on my feet as we zoomed forward. My hands clutched the bar in front of me, and I clenched my jaw as the wind blew my jowls out wide. I kept my eyes closed, but every now and then I forced them open to make sure all was well. In a corner here and there, I would notice a lantern hanging above warning signs that said, "Stay Seated!" in supersized letters. After plummeting abruptly, I bit my tongue and tasted blood. Adrenaline rushed through my veins making me feel prickly in my arms and legs. Voices chattered with excitement when we slowed and I heard the chains lock into place. The metal rollers grinded against the rails with erratic jerks and pulled us up the next steep hill. It was an enjoyable break, but I yearned for more.

"Tell the kids to hang on, ma'am, big drop coming up," the officer told Mom. She turned and repeated his words to us. I couldn't decide if the twins were enjoying the ride so far; Jody's eyes darted from Jessica to me. If I was reading her face correctly, she wanted to know if we were feeling the fear and anxiousness she was feeling. I was not. I anticipated the thrill to come.

Planting my feet firmly, I wiggled my butt flat to the cold vinyl seat before we crested the top. Screaming from the front warned me to prepare for the immediate jolt to high speed again. A brutal whipping action threw me off guard. I wasn't prepared for the upward jerk before the immediate gravity-defying drop! It knocked me loose from the bar. I screamed with my mouth wide open. My body lifted as I grasped the bar, hanging on for dear life, praying the bar would not unlock and pop up. I gradually floated back to my seat, then we swooshed to a glide along the ground rails. I was glad it had been a while since we ate that patty melt; I could hear a few lunches being tossed. Being skinny had its disadvantages; that last plunge almost jarred me out from under the locked bar. *What if the curve to enter the hideaway is so razor-sharp that I fly through the air and hit the wall? Or worst yet, fall onto the tracks?*

I pushed the fear down as the ride intensified, pulling me from my thoughts. We looped first to the right then to the left. It took us upside down for lengthy moments. The velocity pushed me below the bar, down to the floor. A spray of water hit my face. The odd smell made me shiver, as I sure hoped it was just water. I scrambled on the damp floor to get back in my seat. I took a quick moment to look ahead to make sure my sisters were okay. To my surprise, they were peering over the side, looking down below. We were on tracks suspended in the air and a string of lights reflected into the water of a stream or small river, which made me feel better about earlier wetness. We orbited higher and seemed to be encircling the mountain. As we descended, I wondered if we were heading back for the second time through. That was okay with me, I was ready to get off.

I saw the officer motion to Mom, then yell, "*Exito!*" His code word to warn us to hang on, we would enter the secret door to the women's home soon. He moved his arms, showing us to grasp the bar tightly. I closed my eyes and squeezed the bar with all my might, ducking my head just to be safe. I felt a spiky yank to the right and a gust of wind forced my head back; my head popped forward at the very moment the wind stopped. I opened my eyes, wondering if the officer was still there, he wasn't, our single rollercoaster car was the only thing that had entered this corridor through the secret door. We were alone in a long hallway with colors that mimicked the brightly painted walls we had admired on the outside corridor—different scenes but obviously painted by the same person. We all sat stunned, trying to recover from the harrowing ride we had just experienced.

Jessica suddenly blurted out, "Mom, I have to go the bathroom . . . bad!"

We all disembarked to look around. There were no doorways in this small lit-up area, no signs saying, "Ladies room," or, "Exit." Mom heard footsteps and put her hand up to quiet us. An elderly, short, stocky man came running up the

THE SECRET INSIDE BERRYHILL MOUNTAIN

passageway out of the darkness. His mostly bald head was shiny clean and the few strands of hair he had, looked freshly combed across it.

"I'm so sorry," he said over and over as he approached.

"You are just fine," Mom reassured him. "We just got here, I promise."

He seemed relieved as he adjusted the suit he was wearing. It was pretty clear to me that he wasn't accustomed to wearing it. He shook Mom's hand and introduced himself. "My name is Sturgis."

"Nice to meet you, Sturgis," Mom said. Then she introduced all of us, even remembering to call me "Joy."

He greeted us, then said, "Follow me please." His short legs moved fast with the heels of his oversized shoes snapping against the cement floor.

Mom's voice was calm as she caught up to him. "Mr. Sturgis?" she panted, out of breath. He stopped abruptly and turned around with a puzzled look on his face. "We need to use the bathroom." Mom planted her hands firmly on her hips, bucking his rushed attitude.

"No bathroom here." He turned and rushed away. We followed him through the same darkness we had seen him emerge from. He turned on lights revealing what looked like a dead end. Mr. Sturgis fumbled with a panel until a section of wall inched its way open, spastically, as if it was motorized. Light from outside filled the hallway. One by one we filed through; it was a very tight fit for Sturgis, as he had to turn sideways and squeeze himself through. As he let go of the door, it mechanically pulled itself shut and completely blended into the mountainside. We stood staring at it in amazement. Sturgis saw Mom's face became alarmed.

"It's for your protection, ma'am," he reassured.

We stood on a dirt stairway halfway up the mountain. As my eyes adjusted to the light, I looked out over the countryside. A smaller version of Berryhill Amusement Park was down in the valley. I saw a Ferris wheel, bumper cars, a merry-go-round, and a flying scooter ride. Instead of castles, it looked like a quaint, little village. Surrounding the village and amusement park were cute, little bungalow cottages. It had the makings of a picture-perfect place I had read about in fairytales. Cassandra made happy noises as she pointed to the cottages. Each one was unique, a different color and design, donning porches and gardens that encircled around them. The roofs were like none I had ever seen. Some were rounded and covered with red terracotta tiles. Others were wooden with extensions of upper porches wrapped with beautiful railings and hanging baskets. We rode down the mountainside in Sturgis's ten-seated covered cart that reminded me of a supersized golf cart.

"What a beautiful fairytale community this is," Mom told Sturgis.

"Yes, ma'am. Mr. Berryhill thinks everyone should have a place to be proud of."

"Does he live here?" Cassandra asked.

"No, ma'am, he owns homes all over the world. Right now he's in Switzerland. He does come several times a year to check on things. That's why there are strict rules to keep everything perfect. We never know when he might come."

Chapter Six
Our New Home Sweet Home

AFTER FINDING A bathroom, Mr. Sturgis took us on a tour of all the facilities. The city was a perfect circle. Shops and boutiques were in the center with the amusement park wrapping around them. Bungalows surrounded the outside edge in half-circle rows. Row after row, a distinct charm radiated from each home. Each home had a small yard and a very wide sidewalk that curved in front. No mailboxes, no streets, no garages.

"No need," Mr. Sturgis explained. "We don't allow any vehicle larger than this tram."

"No pets either?" Jessica winced.

"No. Occasionally a squirrel or a rabbit will come down from the mountains." He pointed in a semicircle at the mountain range behind the west of the bungalows. "We don't encourage the girls to get attached," he added. "Well, let's get you settled in. Then you can take the girls to get the clothes and things they will need."

We were all excited when Mr. Sturgis took the back path to our bungalow. "This row hasn't been finished long, and you will be the first to be back here." He motioned to a little green two-story cottage halfway down the row. It backed up to a grassy, sloped, ravine area and had a picturesque view of the mountains. "They just got your trees planted this morning, and I have to say you got one of the best floor plans. That extra story adds quite a bit of space."

We all smiled, and I was especially pleased when I saw the porch swing. The porch was large with white railings that fully enclosed the front of the house. The second story had windows across the front and a walkout landing with sliding doors in the back.

"This is where I give you the keys, so to speak." Mr. Sturgis bowed. "You girls enjoy your new place."

Mom stood solemnly at the door, nervous about the prospect of entering. Jessica and Jody had already claimed the swing. Cassandra and I stood behind Mom waiting to go inside. Even though the house was a sage green color, the door was a freshly varnished wood. With a thin row of symmetrical wood panels at the bottom and a full glass pane at the top, it was different from any door I had ever seen. Mom commented on how beautiful and very expensive looking it was. She opened the door and we stepped inside. Straight ahead was the staircase and to the right was a beautiful open room, with the kitchen and living room together. Tall white cabinets covered the back wall and a very long snack bar divided the two areas. Someone must have been planning on company, because five colorful place settings filled the snack bar counter. The living room had two plump, curvy red

THE SECRET INSIDE BERRYHILL MOUNTAIN

couches facing each other, with a center glass coffee table. A brick fireplace covered the front-facing wall up to the door. A bay window was on the other side of the front door, with a wooden built-in eating area.

I plopped down on the couch and sighed. *This was my new home.* I pulled out the pink ribbon and ponytail, then tossed my flip-flops toward the fireplace. Cassandra was going through all the cabinets, proclaiming joy over the abundance of contents. "Peanut butter! Cereal! Two kinds! Popcorn! Apples! A big box of granola bars!" That got the twins' attention, but both were sidetracked by the lure of the stairs.

"Let's run up and call dibs on a bedroom," Jody said, running to the top. I leaped over the coffee table to dart to the stairs. "Mom!" Jody had made it to the top first and spoke down to Mom from the top step.

"Yes, Jody?" Mom answered.

"Two bedrooms?" Jody whined.

"That's all we had at the duplex! We all shared a room!" I reminded as I passed her.

Mom looked around and found a master suite down stairs, soothing Jody's ruffled feathers. "Cassandra and Joey can share; you and Jessica will be fine together."

I called dibs on the room with the sliding glass door and Cassandra seemed pleased. "That upper porch is awesome!" I exclaimed. Normally, this would be when we unpacked and settled in, but we had nothing to unpack, which was the way they wanted it. After going through every drawer and cabinet just to see what was supplied, we were more than shocked. Sheets, towels, dishes, soaps, shampoo and conditioner, deodorant, toothpaste, and electric toothbrushes! Combs, brushes, hair care products, like hairspray and gel—the bathroom cabinet was full. The only thing missing was clothes. Mom said she would hand wash our clothes in the sink and hang dry and we would go tomorrow to the circle of shops to get some clothing. At nine o'clock, we all fell into bed, dog-tired. I closed my eyes and fell asleep with a smile on my face.

    I awoke feeling so happy; this being-a-girl thing was working out so far. The bed was comfortable; the sheets were soft and cozy. I had been relieved of the biggest stress in my young life, worrying about upsetting Tab's applecart! The fear of his temper affecting our lives was over. I didn't have to tiptoe through the house anymore! I could eat at the kitchen table without waiting for him to finish. And the five o'clock panic knowing he would be home soon was over! I figured Mom was feeling the same way!

    As I flew down the stairs to ask Mom if she felt happy, I realized I couldn't. She had brought Tab into our lives and I was sure she felt guilty about that. When I got downstairs, I saw Mom sitting on the porch swing. "Did you sit out here all night, Mom?"

    Mom gasped and turned around. "Oh my goodness. You scared me. No. I washed my clothes and went to bed right after you and the girls. I found some coffee and decided to sit out here and enjoy the morning."

    I sat down next to her, grabbed her hand, and swung

THE SECRET INSIDE BERRYHILL MOUNTAIN

quietly, enjoying the peace and serenity. I leaned back, fully relaxed, and that was when it happened. At eight o'clock sharp, a bell went off, ringing throughout the neighborhood. It wasn't a whimper of a bell; it was loud and it was piercing. Moments later, the sidewalks were full of women and children. Mom and I went back in and shut the door.

Cassandra and the twins stumbled down the stairs staring at Mom as if she was responsible for the bell. Mom raised her hands to clarify. "I have no idea what that was."

"That must be the school bell," Jody speculated after seeing the flow of women and girls strolling down the double-wide sidewalk on the next street. She jumped when a knock came to the door.

"Go up and get dressed," Mom said, as she ushered us to the stairs. We hurried up the stairs, then turned and watched as Mom opened the door. Sturgis stood with his hands clasped, smiling profusely. He was dressed in a slightly more casual outfit, a khaki shirt and shorts, but his few strands of hair still looked freshly combed across his sparkling white bald head.

"Good morning! So glad you are dressed," he said, pleased. "You would not believe how many . . . well, enough of that. Let's go to the village and get you girls some clothes!"

We squealed with excitement as we followed Sturgis.

"Where's the tram?" I asked.

"Walking is good for you!" he said, as he slapped his chest for effect. "They only let me use it to escort new families in," he whispered. My eyebrows raised.

"Or when they leave?" I asked, remembering what Officer Matt Darden had said.

"Oh, it's wonderful here! Nobody wants to leave!" Sturgis replied. I had to agree, so far it had been pretty awesome.

As we walked, Mom asked Sturgis about the bell. "One of the rules," he stated. "At precisely eight o'clock, all girls under eighteen leave for school, and all girls over eighteen leave for work. I will get you a copy of the rules and assign you a job." Mom accepted his premise.

Chapter Seven

Mystery Observer: Friend or Foe

WE TOOK THE long way, walking past every cottage. Sturgis had memorized the names and ages of family members who lived there. "I want to acquaint you with the neighborhood. I think you'll fit in nicely." There were so many names; I didn't know how I would remember them all. There were several Jessica's, only one Jody, and one Cassy (Cassandra), but I was the only Joy. And that suited me fine.

Mom listened closely to every name, watching Sturgis closely as he spoke them. After the very last cottage was identified as Miss Marcia Green and her daughters, Becky and Sadie, Mom stopped and questioned Sturgis, "What about Ruthie Darden? Where does she live?"

Sturgis's white head turned even whiter and he sweated so profusely his freshly combed strands of hair melted down to his forehead. He stuttered and cleared his throat while we waited, and Mom never took her eyes away from his. "She . . . well, she's on a list to go home. They have her in a private area. Do you know her?"

"Well not really," Mom raised her eyebrows realizing she'd miss-spoke, because all residents were supposed to be secret. Mom rambled to cover, "We know someone that knows someone else that knows her. And we don't really even know if they know her." Mom had a tangled web of lies going and Mr. Sturgis looked at her very suspicious of her answer.

"Never heard of her," Sturgis spouted as he turned to walk away. Mom raised her eyebrows again, and her eyes smiled above her puckered lips. We knew she dodged a dart, which could lead to getting kicked out, but not before he confessed Ruthie was there.

Not a soul could be seen anywhere. The amusement park was disconcertingly motionless. As we approached the end of the amusement area, I glanced over my shoulder to get one last look and saw someone running. I stopped and focused my eyes closely. With my own eyes I saw someone crawl inside Rapunzel's tower! Opening my mouth to speak, I stopped myself, realizing there was no need to get things stirred up. Most likely, just a girl skipping school. The shopping was next on our list, and I hated to shop, but I was eager to see the inside of the storefront shops.

The walkway leading to the shops was very unique, it was perfectly placed bricks, three going one way and three going the other. It made for an eye-pleasing rickrack design. Wooden steps and a wooden sidewalk graced the storefront walkways, leading around the circle of shops.

Sturgis led the way to the first shop and I saw Mom sneak up behind him and whisper in his ear. He stopped and turned to look at her. I watched his mouth waiting for words but none came out, he nodded twice and turned around to walk through the door of the shop.

"Miss Hopper, this is Mrs. Randal and her girls. They arrived yesterday." Sturgis politely stepped back and let Mom step forward.

Miss Hopper was slightly older than Mom was. She hugged Mom and each one of us. I could sense she was very kindhearted. I wondered if she knew our story. She didn't wear makeup, but a healthy, natural glow gave her face a fresh, pleasing appearance. I looked around the store and felt panic rise in my throat. My cheeks burned as I gazed upon the rows of panties, bras, and nightgowns. I hadn't considered the fact that I would have to wear girl's undergarments. I stepped out of the store and sat down on the stairs. I heard Mom say, "Joy hasn't been feeling well. I will pick her out a few things."

My face felt warm as I cupped my hands around it. My elbows dug into my knees as I was trying to cope. The walkways were empty and quiet. I wondered how this store, or any store for that matter, could stay in business with no customers. I was in the process of counting to see how many stores there were when I heard a rustling come from under the wooden walkway. I held my breath. Then I heard it again. I moved to lay flat on the second step and peered underneath.

"I know you're under there," I said. The rustling increased. I could see a child's silhouette moving away from me. I watched until she was completely out of sight.

The door to the shop opened and Jody yelled "Joy!" louder than necessary. "Mom said to get up off the ground." I could sense the pleasure Jody had in delivering that scold of a message.

I sat back up and pondered on the silhouette under the porch. Why would this girl be playing hooky? Was she spying on me? Maybe she knew I was a boy. She could be a spy for Mr. Berryhill. Surely I wasn't the first boy who was able to make it in. Fear twisted my stomach. I decided I'd better get back inside and act interested in girl things! Maybe this whole girl thing wasn't going to be as easy as I thought.

"Look, Joy!" Jody held up some matching undergarments as I walked in. "Mom got these for you!"

I approached with a whole new strategy. "Oh, I like those!" I blurted, sounding painfully flamboyant, more so than I had planned. Mom jerked her head around so quickly I heard her neck crack. She gave me a disturbed look as she grabbed the undergarments from Jody and laid them onto the counter. I hid in the corner until the girls were finished.

"The next store is all khaki uniforms," Sturgis informed us. He introduced us to Miss Blackwell. She walked us over to a long wall with various items of clothing, but everything had that same brownish tone. Our complete wardrobe would be khaki uniforms for work, for play, and for school—khaki, khaki, khaki . . .

"Bummer!" Cassandra whined.

"Three months," Mom said softly as she winked.

It took two hours to go through every little shop. I was pleased to find that the shoes gave me a little variance. Black for school and work, but I could wear any kind of shoe I wanted to play in (thankfully, flip-flops were not allowed.) We spent time in every shop and Sturgis introduced us to

THE SECRET INSIDE BERRYHILL MOUNTAIN

more women than I could remember names for. The best store, the Birthday Shop, was next to last on the street. On your birthday, you could pick any one item you wanted! I asked about Christmas, and Sturgis shook his head.

"No. You don't get to pick out your own Christmas gift. Mr. Berryhill brings in some things for everyone."

"Wow!" Cassandra again proclaimed all of our sentiments.

Sturgis found great pleasure in showing us the last shop. The ice cream parlor was pink and blue and had all the charisma of an old-fashioned soda shop. "Once a week, or if you receive a bonus card from work or school, you can turn it in for ice cream." He handed each of us a bonus card. "Special treat from me," he said with a smile.

"Sturgis is turning out to be a pretty swell guy," I told Mom.

"He is," Mom agreed.

We sat at a tall bistro table close to the window with our chocolate cones. I lowered my voice, speaking to Mom, "What did you whisper to Sturgis?"

Mom shrugged as she answered, "I told him we were not a threat to Ruthie."

"Well, I need to tell you guys something . . ." I said mysteriously. "Someone has been following me."

Mom's eyebrows shot up. "Why do you say that?"

I glanced around to make sure no one was listening then leaned forward. "I saw a girl hiding in the amusement park and then again when I was outside the underwear store."

Mom held a breath to keep from laughing, "Undergarments," she said, correcting me.

"Is that why you changed your attitude?" Jody interjected.

"Yes," I said, barely moving my lips. "I thought I better throw them off!"

Mom laughed then grew serious. "We do need to stay in character as much as possible. Getting kicked out would put us in quite a tough spot."

I leaned back, knowing Mom was right. We were here to keep her safe, to keep us safe, away from Tab.

Sturgis pulled up with the cart and began loading all of our new things. "That's a bit much to carry," he justified his use of the cart. "I will set it inside your door."

Mom was grateful, "Thank you, Sturgis."

We stayed at the ice cream parlor and Mom made friends with Gilda. She and Mom hit it off immediately. We heard the twenty-minute version of her life story, and I was enthralled with her pixie-like face, that matched her haircut as she spoke. No children or family, just an abusive boyfriend who wanted her dead. He went to jail, but three years ago he'd escaped from prison and made it his life's mission to finish the job. Gilda showed us rope burn scars from being left in his basement. She was his prisoner for months until she was able to slip her thinned arms through the ropes he had tied her up with.

She was still very thin, and I had no clue how she managed it working so close to all the ice-cream. She loved living here; her house was on the street behind the north shops. She worked at the ice cream parlor most days, but was hoping to become a substitute teacher at the school when they needed her. Being a former schoolteacher, she had her name in for a full-time position. She showed us how to get to the school and with a word of caution she said, "Be ready to walk out that door when you hear the eight o'clock bell ring, they have no tolerance for late-ness here!" The stern-ness of her warning made me think she knew more than she was saying.

We made our way home without stopping. Mom was quiet as the girls discussed Gilda, "That is so … so … h-o-r-r-i-b-l-e …" Jessica said, exaggerating her words.

"She is lucky to be alive!" Jodie said nodding, "Her boyfriend is evil!"

Mom was smiling, so I knew she wasn't listening to the twins. "What are you smiling about, Mom?" I asked. Her smile was exuding happiness, I found myself smiling,

"Oh I was thinking how happy Matt will be to see his mom. Sturgis said she's in a separate area preparing to go home. Matt thought we would be giving his mother Ruthie a message and now looks like he will be the one to deliver the message. I think that will be a wonderful day for both of them."

That took over the discussion as Cassandra joined in, "Eight years that is way too long to not see a mother!"

"Yea!" The twins added, grabbing one each of Mom's arms. "That would be way too hard! I wouldn't wait that long to see you Mom!" Mom stooped to hug them.

I was scheming to get over to the amusement park, and thought I would ask while Mom was so happy, but she wasn't going for it, at least not today. I kept glancing at Rapunzel's tower. When I had a chance that would be my first destination.

Just as Sturgis had said, the multiple boutique bags were neatly placed inside the door. Mom was hoping to run into him again, to make sure he understood why we were not a threat to Ruthie.

Mom delegated work for each of us. The twins and I would put away all the new things and she and Cassandra would start dinner. Mom was a good cook, at least by our standards. Her macaroni and cheese was the best.

Mom and I sat by the fireplace while Cassandra and the twins washed the dishes. We could see children playing on the next street. Mom asked if we wanted her to walk us over to meet some of them, but no one took her up on it. We preferred spending time with Mom. At the duplex, Tab had taken up most of her time. The only saving grace, if we had one. Tab left for work at five in the morning, and most nights he was in bed by seven-thirty. When the season allowed, Mom would sit outside and watch us play. During the dark winter months, we had to sit perfectly quiet on the couch. If we moved, we had to do it silently. Tab's voice put the fear of God in us. We were not allowed to eat with Tab; we stayed upstairs until he finished. He had his moments though. I remembered an occasional Saturday night when he was in a good mood. He would toss a handful of change across the floor for us kids to gather and keep. We would wait until Mom and Tab went out for the evening, then Cassandra would take us down to the gas station—that was the only time we indulged in pop and candy.

I vaguely remembered any of my grandparents except for Mom's mom, Martha King Brown. She stayed with us for a while. King was her maiden name, and she used it as her middle name. It came down the line from her grandfather, Choctaw Chief Eugene King. She was the one that instilled a love for my heritage. She was a quiet woman, but told wonderful stories about her father and grandfather's lives. She believed in prayer, and I could hear her praying for Mom and us kids, and even Tab, through the bathroom door. The bathroom was the only private place we had and Grandma Brown spent a lot of time inside it reading her bible. Mom and Tab fought over her being there and she went back to California. She gave us a huge white family sized bible with colorful pictures of bible heroes, before she left. A few weeks later it disappeared and the house never felt the same. Cassandra finally told me Tab tossed it in the attic.

Chapter Eight
Girl Lesson 101

AT SIX A.M., the lights popped on. My stomach was in full swing quivering mode at the thought of being a girl in front of a class full of girls. Mom found the rules pamphlet Sturgis gave her and read it aloud while we ate breakfast. The clock was approaching 7:00 when Mom instructed us to dress and be at the front door by 7:55. It took a little longer being a girl. I had to wait for Cassandra to dress so she could help me fix my hair. Pink didn't go well with khaki, so we found a black plastic headband and pushed the bulk of my hair back. Khaki shorts and khaki shirt, I sure hoped it wasn't a mistake wearing shorts, it sure showcased my big, knobby knees.

Cassandra took me out to the back balcony for some "Girl" lessons. "Joey walk across the porch."

"My name is Joy!" I said sarcastically. I moved a little slow and prissy, hoping this lesson would be short and sweet. After all I have lived side-by-side with girls my whole life!

"That's good, but cut back on the hip swing. It looks fake."

I tried again, with less swing. Mom slid the door open.

"Oh! You look great Joy, I thought you were a girl out here! Thank you Cassandra for working with him."

Cassandra beamed, "Maybe I'll be a teacher someday!"

I patted Cassandra's shoulder as I passed her going through the sliding door, "That's fine, just don't tell your class who your first student was . . ."

I stood by the door at 7:45. The twins came next. Cassandra rushed in at 7:58. Mom ushered us out to the porch, planting a big kiss on our foreheads, moments before the sound of the bell. We had made it! We cut between the next streets cottages and intercepted a group of girls heading to the east. A cement sidewalk led to the south end of the mountain. *This could be interesting*, I thought. *A school inside the mountain?* School had always been an escape for me. A place I could blend in and be normal, speak in my full voice and walk as loud as I wanted. The sights and smells of school had become comforting. The crayons and the chalkboard, the 10:30 aroma of hot, buttery, rolls coming from the cafeteria. Seeing the kids having fun at recess through the long row of windows. It gave me hope there was more to life than setting on the couch and being told to stay quiet.

The farther we walked, the more fascinated I became. There were no doors or windows. Six women could be seen in the distance. All were smiling, except one older lady who reminded me of a mad Bulldog. Her mouth turned down instead of up and with a distinct under bite her bottom teeth were visible. Her hair on top was tightly curled to her head and she had bobby pins pulling the sides up. Her skin was pale and she wore no make-up at all. She spoke to the women as our group approached.

"Ladies you have a nice day and please accomplish your work assignments for the day." A door popped open after she pushed several buttons and the women all walked in without speaking. The door was slammed shut, and she turned her attention to us.

"Good morning, girls, my name is Miss Barrett. Please stand in a straight line until I take a head count."

Her voice was deep and gruff and matter of fact, we formed a straight line, just as we were told, while Miss Barrett counted each head. My legs certainly stood out among the others so while we jostled for single file positions, I meandered to the back of the line. We stood for at least five minutes more, before a keypad was revealed and four numbers were pushed. The same section of mountain that the women went through, the size of a door popped loose as it unlocked, then sluggishly opened in a power-driven manner. All the teachers were dressed in identical khaki, and nodded at each girl as she passed through the opening. Miss Barrett stood behind the others and looked down our line. I watched her face, as it instantly took on an ugly frown, and became irritated. Grunting, she stretched over to the still open panel to press a button. The shrill sound that proceeded scared the living daylights out of me. I covered my ears, shrinking in fear, convinced that I had been discovered.

When I heard and felt no one, I opened my eyes. Three teachers, led by Miss Barrett, were almost to the end of our walkway, running toward a young girl. The scraggly, red haired girl in dirty khaki's was darting back and forth, but was blocked by a large man. She crawled across the ground trying to escape. The women reached her and yells of anger erupted. The big man was partially blocking my view; but Miss Barrett was bent over the girl on a yelling rampage. I was pushed inside and the door shut. I caught up with the girls and wondered if my sisters had witnessed any part of the aggressive waylay I had seen.

We followed a hallway that ended at the mountain's edge. We entered a room to the east and I was glad to see a row of windows looked out over the valley to the south. The two remaining teachers came in and acted as if nothing had happened. I watched for some explanation—none was given.

The class sat down, leaving Cassandra and I standing there looking awkward. I knew we were thinking the same thing: *Are we all in the same class?* The answer soon became apparent. Yes, all ages would be taught together. The morning lessons seemed the same as any school: reading, writing, and math. We had a thirty-minute lunch break and I squeezed between the twins, who sat across from Cassandra. "Is this weird or what, me being in your class?" I asked, looking at Cassandra.

"I kinda like it," Jody said.

"It's not bad," Cassandra added. "Better than being cooped up in small rooms."

"My teacher said we will be sewing!" Jessica said, throwing her arms onto the mottled gray Formica table, joyously tapping her fingers.

"That's great," Cassandra encouraged.

I leaned forward and focused in on Cassandra, whispering loudly, "I guess we know why Gilda warned us not to be late! That girl on the sidewalk was late and she was in big trouble!"

"You think the alarm went off because someone was late?" Cassandra asked.

I nodded profusely, "I'm pretty sure she got a spanking." Cassandra stretched her eyes in disbelief. Two teachers stood behind Cassandra listening, so I dropped the matter.

Lunch was over and we moved to a separate part of the school. The large room had three distinct areas and was divided only by large open walkways. Signs above, told the activity to be done there, "Cooking," "Sewing," and "Fabric Preparation." A kitchen lined the north side, with desks facing a long counter that was covered with the same mottled gray Formica as the lunchroom. The center section had rows of sewing machines surrounded by worktables. The third area had bolts of fabric, washers and dryers, and dozens of ironing boards.

The three teachers who had greeted us that morning and chased down the little girl entered the room. This time we were divided up into groups by age, thus my sisters and I were separated. Cassandra, along with ten or twelve girls her age, were taken to the bolts of fabric. Jessica and Jody were seated at sewing machines. I panicked, as I was left in the kitchen area, but I didn't complain when I realized the alternative, was sewing or ironing.

We were taught in a very carefree manner and even though I was nervous about being discovered as a boy, I was kinda interested in learning to cook. The teacher read from a booklet describing the various ways to cook. We watched her demonstrate the process you would follow to bake, boil, fry and broil, then we divided into smaller groups for hands on experience. My group made cornbread, and each one of us had to stand in front and tell the steps we followed. Halfway through my turn, someone commented on my big kneecaps. I tugged on my shorts, glad I had paid attention to the recipe. I continued talking with my best girl voice, "Stir the eggs and milk into the cornmeal mix, then pour the mixture into an 8 inch greased pan, bake it at 400 degrees for 40 minutes."

The teacher complimented me nicely. "That was very good, Joy." I smiled and pushed my black headband back into place.

When I turned to go to my seat, I made a point to see how Cassandra and the twins were doing. Cassandra was holding up a piece of fabric she had cut and was on her way to the ironing board. The twins were listening closely to the teacher, who was reading a section from *The Art of Sewing*. She held the book up in demonstration. My thoughts rambled, examining all the girls. *Did all these girls have abusive dads—with no brothers?* I gazed around the room, scrutinizing everyone. There weren't any boys, except me.

Homework was not a part of this school! I danced on the inside hearing those words. When our three afternoon teachers stood and gave final instructions, I wanted so badly to ask what had happened to that little girl this morning, but it didn't seem appropriate. Which was nothing like Jefferson Middle School. You could ask anything you wanted, as long as you held up your hand first. The whole atmosphere seemed strange. I couldn't pinpoint why, but it didn't feel like school. Thankfully, it was over and I had other things on my mind. We filed back to the entrance, passing only five teachers. From a distance, they looked identical as they stood next to each other—short curly hair, no makeup, and black shoes protruding from their long khaki skirts. We waited until the button was pushed and then politely walked down the sidewalk. Robots came to mind. No sweat off my back; tomorrow was Saturday and I had big plans.

I went to bed early with instructions to not wake me up because I was planning to sleep in. I asked God to forgive me as I stomped up the stairs. I had no plans on sleeping in; I had to get to the amusement park before it opened. I tucked all my clothing under my pillow and took a few extra pillows from the linen closet to use as my body double during my defection.

It was still dark when I awoke. The clock said 5:08. I dressed and made my body double. (I lined the three pillows under my blankets). I did surveillance as I ate a small bowl of corn flakes, missing my Fruity Pebbles. After observing the sidewalks being empty, I went back upstairs and out through the sliding glass door. I carefully climbed down the trellis. Feeling pretty proud of myself, I smiled nonstop as I crawled across the sidewalks, making it past three rows of houses. I wasn't sure how I was going to explain my knees being so dirty, but I was thankful I had found the old clothes I had come here with.

Once I got close to the park, I made a mad dash, gliding through the grass and landing flat on the ground. I turned sideways and pulled myself through the gates, which had a loose chain holding them together. The ticket and emergency shelter was dark and empty. I passed two toddler rides, then stopped at the House of Mirrors and waited. Once I was convinced I hadn't been seen, I looked for the best way to get to my destination—Rapunzel's tower. There was no easy way to get there, because it was beyond a large open walkway. I grumbled in frustration; it was already starting to get light outside. I took my stance, gearing up for another mad dash when I heard something. I backed up and stood very quiet. My ears were large and worked better than most. I had no reason to doubt myself. The girls laughed when Mom swore that I could hear a pin drop in the house next door.

I heard it again, nothing loud, just a faint sniffle. Someone was inside the House of Mirrors. I took off my shoes and tiptoed inside a small entry room. I warned myself to be prepared to see the walls full of distorted mirrors, before going in. I knew I needed to perceive things judiciously. My preparedness, sure didn't work. My heart raced after witnessing a ten-foot, big head version of myself.

I followed the flow of rooms, not seeing or hearing anything, no one was here—at least not in plain view. I put on my shoes and circled the outside, going back to the front. Standing in the doorway, I paused to listen. There was the sound again, a slight sniffle of the nose. It came from the right side, and as far as I could tell, there was no entrance that way. I bent down and peeked through a small shelf. I saw feet, legs, arms, and elbows all squished into a small cubical, no bigger than sixteen inches tall. It was a child. I pondered for a moment on what to do. I didn't want to scare her or give her a chance to run. I had worked too hard to find her.

"Don't be afraid," I whispered softly, then listened

carefully to see if my subtleness had worked.

"Who are you?" she said with a shuffle, as if she was shifting to a position to see me.

"My name is Joy." A pause ensued.

"How did you know I was here?" the voice said, sounding a little uneasy.

"I saw you yesterday... twice actually."

"You saw me?"

"Well, I saw you run into the Rapunzel's tower, and I saw someone under the stairs, by the boutique. Was that you?"

"Uh-huh. I'm stuck in here. Can you come around and help me get out?" She told me to go back out front and follow to the left where there was a small storage cabinet connected to the cubby she had crawled inside of. I opened the storage door and hunkered down to see her face. I pushed her head down and pulled her toward me. She plopped out and sprawled onto the ground, clutching her legs in pain. She was a freckle-faced girl around ten, who looked as if her matted red hair had never been brushed. She stretched each leg out and sat up. She then glared at me, raising her long fingernails up as if she wanted to scratch my eyes out.

"You don't need to worry about me," I quickly said. "We just got here and I'm trying really hard to stay out of trouble."

She backed down from her soon-to-attack mode, but kept her eyes on mine. "Are you the new family that moved into that green house, way to the back?"

"Yes." I stuck out my hand, but she shook her head.

"No!" she said forcefully. This girl was like none I had ever seen. She seemed like a wounded animal! She moved around as if she was in pain.

"Are you hurt?" I asked.

"Well, I got away before they hurt me bad, I acted like a rabid animal and they let me go. But Miss Barrett got me with her long fingernails. She scratched me bad!" She lifted her shirt to reveal deep red scratches. "Miss Barrett and her crew spend most of their time trying to catch me. I always get away," she beamed, wearing that statement as a badge of honor.

"That was you on the school sidewalk yesterday, wasn't it?"

"Yes," she slurred, begrudgingly. "I was trying . . . well, sometimes if I get to the door in time, I can wedge my fingers inside to keep it from shutting. Then I pull it back open after the teachers go down the hall. I get food from the lunch room."

She glanced outside; it was daylight. "I have to get to Rapunzel's tower!" she shouted. I wanted to ask her name, but the urgency in her voice told me no time.

"Will I see you again?" I blurted out quickly.

"After dark I come back here." She stopped and turned around. "And don't you tell a soul!"

"I won't. I promise!" I looked at her sincerely when I said it, moving my hands to cross my heart. Her eyes altered and with a slight smile her large dimples became prominent—she believed me. I watched as she moved like a gazelle, leaping over, under, and across anything in her way. Working my way back to our street, I saw a few people who waved at me from their porch. That gave me a little hope; maybe a few normal people lived here. So far, it felt as though I'd fallen down a hole like, *Alice in Wonderland*.

Mom was on the porch reading. I didn't have the wherewithal to sneak back up the trellis. I felt sad and depressed. The very thing we had run from was happening to people here. Mom pulled down the paper from her face, surprised to see me. "I didn't see you come out," she said. Before I could answer, she looked at my clothes. "What in the world?" She dropped her jaw and the paper at the same time. She stood up and stared at me, at a loss for words.

"I'm sorry, Mom. I got up early to go out and play. I thought my old clothes would be better."

Her face softened, telling me that she scrapped her plan of scolding me. "Well, I'm glad you didn't have your new clothes on."

I received the same reaction as I passed the girls to go upstairs. Standing in the shower, the hot water felt good until it hit my kneecaps. I scoured them with the soap, knowing they would feel better after the initial sting. Behind the bathroom mirror I found everything I needed: Iodine, peroxide, and band-aids. This place might have a few faults, but someone was pretty clever. Every drawer and cabinet was full of anything and everything a person might need should they be injured. I put away the extra pillows and fell into my bed.

Chapter Nine
Where's Sturgis?

"JOEY, WAKE UP."

My feet instinctively rose to my chest when I realized Jody and Jessica were tickling the back of my foot to wake me. I rolled over feeling hot and drowsy, but forced my eyes open when I heard them speaking. "Mom said we can go to the amusement park now!" They spoke in a synchronized harmony.

"Really?" I said, sitting straight up. I cheered inside until I remembered the little red-haired girl.

Mom was exiting our upstairs bathroom. "As soon as you get that bathtub clean!" She held up a bottle of Mr. Clean and a sponge. I jumped up, pulling the sheet around me, and ran to get my clothes. "Make your bed too!" she added, descending down the stairs.

The amusement park was in full operational mode. The sounds made me feel jittery. I tried to decide if that was good or bad. It brought back fond memories of the two hours of fun we had in the Berryhill Amusement Park before gliding into this secret home. But I couldn't get past the cocklebur of knowing a frightened little girl was hiding somewhere in here with a story I wanted to know, and it was all I could think about.

We walked through the gate, stopping at the ticket counter to read the sign. "Open all day Saturday and Sunday. All Children under 12 must be accompanied by an Adult."

"Shoot!" I muttered.

Jessica looked at me. 'Two days isn't enough?" I pointed to the "under 12" part. "Oh," she said dismissively, as she walked off.

It was by no means the same stature as Berryhill Amusement Park, but it would do with smaller versions of the rides. We looked in vain for a Castle Slide, which had created a highpoint in our family. Mom said, "Well, a small one wouldn't have been the same. And, anyway, we can remember the Castle Slide as a special experience, one we will have again someday."

Mom was right; nothing that would fit in here could compare, and the thought of the someday she spoke of gave me joy. Surprisingly a large number of people were here. I looked at every face, screening for freckles and red hair. The girl must have family here—a mother she came in with. It wasn't possible to walk in off the street.

We rode the bumper cars and it took my thoughts to a better place for a while. I was pleased with the way my specially picked red car darted in and out of traffic better than most. Cassandra whizzed by with a warning, "Are you driving like a girl, Joy?" I was driving like an animal, having briefly forgotten. The rules for every ride was that you had to exit to get back on. After my driving exhibition, the red car was the most sought ride. That left me with a lackluster yellow beast, which stalled intermittently. I was a target, being hit by all.

We moved past the pond and Rapunzel's Tower was coming up. It was a tall sphere, with a separated musical section on top that turned the lengthy swings hanging to the ground. It played pleasant harpsichord music while the swings flew through the air. It only went fast enough for the swings to glide out and around the musical turnstile. I looked for the red-haired girl as we traveled in a circle around the tower. The very top had a decorative wrought-iron design tall enough for a person to hide behind, although, I didn't think she could stand up inside. My imagination ran wild with thoughts of the little girl staying at the top of the tower and hiding all day. Not a very good life she was living and the matted hair and scratches on her back were more than enough evidence to prove that case.

I wondered if she would be there tomorrow, or would she move to a new, safer place? She would relocate if she feared I would tell someone where she was. Keeping this secret from Mom was wrong, but I would never reveal the girl's hiding places, even if someone threatened to beat me on the back, as I envisioned they did her.

After three turns on Rapunzel's tower, we backtracked to the benches overlooking the pond. Jessica and Jody coaxed a family of ducks with treats from the automated machine. Gilda, the woman at the ice cream parlor, walked by and greeted us as if we were old friends. We walked with her and circled back to the ice cream parlor. This was a true miracle; ice cream twice in three days. Mom sat at the counter with

Gilda, while we kids sat in a booth. The twins and I decided to try the pistachio-flavored ice cream, but after biting into several green nuts, I realized it was a bad choice. The place was full today. They didn't sell food at the park, except to feed the ducks, but when you exited, you could use your coupon for ice cream.

When we walked home, Mom's demeanor had changed. Cassandra noticed also and asked her what she and Gilda talked about. "They fired Sturgis," she blurted. Her expression revealed that she was clearly shaken. We gasped and looked at her for more information. "He broke the rules is all anyone was told. Gilda was heart-broken. He was the go-between for the women here and Mr. Berryhill. He was their advocate."

"Will they replace him?" Cassandra asked.

"Oh, they already have—the head teacher is taking over."

"What's her name?" I probed quickly.

"Gilda said her name was Miss Barrett. She's the administrator of the teaching department and has been here the longest."

"That's bad..." I said, curling my face in distress.

Mom looked at me funny. "Do you know her?"

"We met her yesterday." The scowl on my face left them waiting for me to clarify. "A little girl was late to school and she got it bad from some of the teachers. Miss Barrett was in charge."

"You mean when the alarm went off?" Cassandra asked.

"Yes," I said, wondering how I was going to back that up with evidence. I ravaged my brain, trying to think of a way to tell them what had happened and yet not tell the secret of the little red-haired girl. "They were too rough on her, Mom!" I finally blurted out. Mom's hand covered her mouth as she looked at me in disbelief. I nodded my head. "They're mean."

"Where does that little girl live, Joey?" Cassandra asked.

I shrugged my shoulders. "I just happened to see her and she looked like she was hurting. When I asked her what was wrong, she showed me her scratched up back." I almost regretted telling Mom and the girls that part, because it sure changed the mood. A dark cloud had invaded our festive Saturday. We took the long way and walked down every sidewalk with strict instruction that I would let Mom know if I saw the little red-haired girl. Of course I wouldn't see her, because she hid in Rapunzel's tower during the day and the House of Mirror's at night. But I had to play along to hide the "secret." I was relieved I had not broken my promise to my newest friend and glad I told the facts that needed to be known. The woman who took over for Sturgis was not a good person to be running things.

We sat quiet and tried to enjoy the rest of the evening on the porch. When the sun went down, everyone disappeared into their houses. I assumed it was because the loud warning bell would go off shortly and the lights would be turned off. I had my own concerns and the decision I needed to make: Did I go back into the amusement park tonight or wait till morning? I feared being caught outside past the curfew. It didn't bother the teachers to punish her; they would surely do the same to me.

"What time is it, Mom?" I asked.

"Almost 8:50," Cassandra answered.

"The curfew is upon us, ten minutes to go girls." I laughed.

"No curfew on the weekend, honey." Mom patted my leg and smiled.

"Oh, well I like that!" I laughed again. I excused myself and went to the kitchen to stuff my pockets with some food. I wasn't sure when this red haired girl had last eaten, but I wanted to be prepared. Taking my stash to bed, I would wait to make the final decision on when to go after I saw what time the girls went to bed. If it was early enough for me to sneak out tonight, I would. If not, I would wait until morning.

Chapter Ten
Face-To-Face Reality

BY 9:15, MOM and the girls were in bed and all lights were out. Being someone who planned ahead, I had gone to bed fully prepared just in case. With my pockets full of granola bars and a bottle of water, I was up and out the glass door by 9:30. I slid down the trellis, which was a little harder with my pockets bulging. Moving from house to house for cover, I strategically made my way to the gate. I squeezed through the chain and waited by the ticket counter until I knew I hadn't been followed. Before I reached our designated meeting place, the House of Mirrors, I heard a whistle, then a voice that said, "Hey, kid . . ." I stopped to see where it was coming from. The ride to the south was the bumper cars, and I saw a head poking up from the farthest car. She pointed to a small house across the way from her; I squatted low and walked like a duck (no knee damage tonight). The sign said, "Barbie's Playhouse." I opened the door, but it was so dark I just stood there.

"Come in," she said, as a flicker of a light showed her face. I wondered how she appeared there so quickly. "Follow me," she urged.

We climbed up a short staircase, the dim light revealed a fully furnished playhouse with child size furniture. We passed a bedroom, "Do you sleep here?" I asked.

"Sometimes. It's a little too obvious, to be a really good hiding place, so I usually sleep in the House of Mirrors or Rapunzel's tower." We went down the hall and into a center closet that had no windows. She shut the door. Cupped in her hands was a small candle that flickered but had no flame. "Battery," she informed me. We sat down opposite each other and she put the candle in the center. "What's all that in your pockets," she asked.

"Granola bars and water. I wasn't sure if you had food."

"Only when I make it into the school," she said grabbing all three in one swipe. She motioned for the water. "Thank you," she said before washing the granola down. "I was starving, I dig through the trash if I can get to it before they pick it up. That's how I knew where you lived. I saw lights and peeked in the window." I just nodded as I listened. "Your trash had some macaroni and cheese." My face went stoic as I wondered why Mom would have thrown any of that away. "It was really good," she said in a business-like manner.

I smiled, because I knew mom makes the best macaroni and cheese. I stared at her red hair. It looked like she had made an attempt to comb some of the knots out, and she actually looked clean revealing her mass of freckles.

"I cleaned up in the fountain and Barbie has a vanity with combs and brushes," she said when she saw me looking. I knew there was important stuff we should be talking about, but I wanted her to finish eating. When she finished the third granola bar, she said, "What's your name?"

"Joey," I said, taking a risk, telling her the truth.

"Well, Joey, you will be sorry you came in this women's home."

I looked her over and evaluated her statement, then decided to start with asking her what I have been wondering ever since I first saw her, "Don't you have a family here? What's your name?"

"My name is Matilda, but call me Mattie. I have a family . . . somewhere. My grandma brought me in here to protect me from them." She went into the long version I could see she thought was a black mark on her life.

"My mother was only sixteen when she had me. A year or so after I was born, my grandma took me because she thought I was in danger. My mom and dad loved me, but my grandma said, 'The lure of drugs towered over everything in their lives, including me." She paused for a moment with a look of antipathy, she took a deep breath and continued. "My parents tried a bunch of times to steal me back from Grandma. That's when my uncle arranged for me and Grandma to come to this place. To be honest, I don't even remember my mom and dad. I was only two when we came here and that was eight years ago. But me and Grandma were happy for a long time, she was the head teacher for a while. Then one day, Grandma made up her mind she was going to the office to get permission for us to go visit her son. That's when our happy world fell apart." Mattie's face took on pure sadness; I could see she had replayed that day many times.

"My grandma overheard a private conversation between Miss Barrett and a big man. They are stealing money and changing the books to hide it. My grandma said they are making more clothes than Mr. Berryhill knows about and selling them behind his back too... Anybody who knows my grandma, knows she breaks no rules. She told em' 'My son the police officer might want to hear about your money stealing scheme!' Well, anyway ... They took away my grandma's position as head teacher and moved her to the clothes manufacturing."

I listened to a story that sounded like a scary movie. They pushed Mattie's grandma to the edge of her health with long hours of work, then with intimidations of no food delivery. Finally, neither were allowed inside the school and office area. When none of that worked, Barrett placed Mattie with another family and no one has seen her grandma since. Mattie had been searching for her grandma day and night until Barrett put a stop to it. After Mattie told them she wouldn't quit looking for her grandma, they came one night to get her. So she ran. She had been on the run, narrowly escaping capture ever since. I hadn't moved a muscle since Mattie started her life story, and of what was going on in this secret women's home. I took a drink of her water and sat awestruck because she was expressive and animated when she spoke. I was exhausted from the high-strung listening.

She leaned in and lowered her voice. "This is the summation of what you need to know: This is not a safe place. My grandma realized the people in charge needed all these women to stay here to make all the clothes."

Those words and the look on this scraggly red haired girls face told me, this was bigger than she and I should be trying to settle. "We need to tell my mom. She's already been worried about you."

Mattie's mouth opened and her forehead wrinkled. "What do you mean? Does your mom know about me?"

"Yea ... well not really you ... she knows Miss Barrett was mean to a little red haired girl. We walked by every house looking for you--because she was concerned you were hurt."

"You promised you wouldn't tell! Does your mom know I'm here?" Mattie rose to her feet.

"No! I didn't tell anyone you were hiding in the park! I just told Mom and the girls about the teachers attacking you at the end of the school sidewalk." I perched my hands on my hips, "I saw that with my own eyes, you know!"

She sat back down, twisting her lips and piercing her blue eyes into mine, to see if I was being truthful.

I held my eyes firm till she spoke. "Has your mom started her job yet?"

"No." I said.

"Well when she does, she will understand. In the past six months the quota has been doubled. My grandma, before she went missing was working seven days a week."

When I got home, Mom was waiting for me. She knew I had left and was waiting not-so-patiently for me to get back. She rarely got mad, and although I had received two spankings in my life, none had come from Mom. In fact she stood nose to nose with Tab after he spanked me for hiding in the trash can, where I had hid during a game of hide and seek. I can still remember her slow, precise words to him as her mad face bulldozed close to his. "You touch any of my kids again and I'm walking out that door ..." The other one came in third grade from Mr. Cox, the Jefferson elementary principal, after three of us boys giggled at our homeroom teacher's strong perfume. In spite of all that, as I climbed the trellis, I felt a little sick to my stomach. Pulling myself over the balcony's edge, Mom cleared her throat. I looked up and the girls were standing behind her in their robes. My guess was they had been up for some time. Mom flipped on a flashlight and pointed for me to sit down. I could see she was more scared than angry and that made me feel bad. I knew I'd better come up with something really good, and the truth was the only really good thing I could think of.

"I found that little girl."

Mom's demeanor changed. She pulled a chair close to sit in front of me. "You mean that's where you've been? You went out looking for her?"

"Yes," I said. It was only half of the story, but it truly was the prominent reason I had gone out of the house.

"Is she all right?" Cassandra asked.

"She is scared and . . ." I stopped and looked at Mom. "She made me promise not to tell anyone. I crossed my heart, Mom." In spite of Tab's bad temper causing her to lie to him, Mom had always taught us to be honest. If Mom said it, she would do it. I knew she could understand my dilemma.

"Joey . . . you need to tell me where she is, sometimes when safety is involved we have to break a promise." My hands were sweating as I mulled things over in my head. Mom continued with her persuasion. "Let me give you an example: let's say hypothetically a bully was being mean to Cassandra every day and she made you promise not to tell anyone. But you knew in your heart there was a better chance he would hurt her if you didn't get her some help. Wouldn't you tell someone?"

That story was a little too close to home and my eyes filled with tears. Mom cupped her hands around mine and squeezed. "Joey..."

I sat up straight. "I would, Mom. I couldn't let anything happen to her." I knew Mom was right; this girl didn't know us. We were on her side and her safety was our only goal. I would tell Mom and the girls all Mattie had told me in confidence and hoped someday she would forgive me.

Chapter Eleven
Full Disclosure

MOM AND THE girls listened as I started off with a warning. "This is not as we thought. She was not being punished for tardiness; she was trying to get away, she's been on the run for a while." Mom gasped. I continued, knowing this complicated story was going to be a hard thing to swallow. "Her name is Mattie, and her grandmother brought her here when she was little. Her parents were taking drugs and couldn't take care of a baby, but they kept trying to kidnap her even though a court order gave her grandmother custody." I looked at Mom. "Mom, we may have made a mistake."

"About what?" she queried.

"Mattie's grandmother figured out that Miss Barrett is stealing money from Mr. Berryhill."

Mom had a thoroughly mixed-up look on her face. "You mean the Miss Barrett they just put in charge?"

I bobbed my head. "Yes, she is the ringleader and she is making the women work hard to have more clothes to sell. Mattie said you will see what she means when they put you to work."

Before Mom could speak, words came flooding out of Cassandra's mouth. "This could be a dangerous web of criminals, like the mafia or something . . . Someone needs to tell Mr. Berryhill."

As I listened to what Cassandra was saying, Mom cleared her throat in an interrupting manner, "Let's not blow this into something scary."

I could see the twins were falling asleep. I decided I'd better tell Mom the worst part in private. Mom put the twins to bed and convinced Cassandra to get some sleep. I was down in the kitchen looking for a snack when Mom came down.

"Mom, I didn't finish the whole story. Do you want me to wait until morning?" She knew me, and knew it was bothering me. I needed to talk about it. She led me to her room and shut the door. The stress of it all finally took its toll and I burst into tears. "Mom," I said as I used my shirt to wipe my nose. "What Mattie told me is so bad."

Mom put her arms around me tightly. "We are gonna help her, Joey."

I pulled back and looked her in the eyes. "They took her grandmother."

Mom had a look of apprehension. "Is that what she told you?"

"Yes. After her grandmother overheard them talking about their secret stuff."

Mom sat back. "Tell me word for word what she said."

"After they lived here for a long time, her grandma wanted to visit her son. She was going to Mr. Berryhill's office to demand they let her call him, and that's when she overheard Miss Barrett and a stranger strategizing. She told

Mattie they were talking about how this non-profit clothing business was making them millions of dollars. They caught Mattie's grandma listening and were mad she heard them. They told her she better stay silent or else she would regret it. But she wasn't going to. She demanded they let her and Mattie leave. She was gonna tell her son everything. Mattie said they made life miserable for her grandma and she still wouldn't back down. One day they came and took Mattie's grandmother, and they left Mattie with another family. She hasn't seen her grandmother since. That's why Mattie ran away; she is looking for her grandmother."

Mom's face paled. "Joey, I need to see and talk to Mattie."

"I know, Mom, only she doesn't trust anyone."

"You tell her I will keep her secret and help find her grandmother."

I wasn't sure how I felt about it, but answered, "I will ask her again."

Mom hugged me. "I am very proud of you, Joey."

I slept in Mom's room. She said it would be best, and there would be no more sneaking out tonight.

I'd slept late the next morning. I went to the kitchen and could sense Mom had told the girls. The mood was bleak. Even though I was the only one eating breakfast, everyone sat at the table with me. Cassandra finally broke the silence. "Could you tell us about her, Joey? Is Mattie scared?"

It surprised me to hear Cassandra call Mattie by her

name. So far she and the twins had known her as "that girl." The answer to the first part of that question would take some thought, but the premise of "was she scared" was a little easier. "She doesn't seem scared. In fact, when I first met her, I was the scared one. I got the feeling that if she saw me as a threat, she would have scratched my eyes out!"

The twins sat back and widened their eyes. "I'm sure after being on her own, she had to toughened herself up just to survive," Mom said, coming to her defense. I agreed with Mom.

"She is very strong physically," I continued. "I saw her move like some kind of superhero. She was fast and agile, moving over and under things like they weren't even there. And boy is she smart. She's the smartest ten-year-old I have ever met. She talks like an adult, with big words and well thought-out stuff. I bet she's the smartest one in this place. One thing she said was; she only gets to eat when she finds food or makes it through the school door to get some from the cafeteria. The day they almost caught her, that's where she was going. She catches the door right before it shuts and just waits until the coast is clear to pull it open. She goes through the neighborhood trash if she gets really hungry." I grinned at Mom. "She found your macaroni; she said it was really good." Mom half smiled before a look of sadness melded.

I explained how I had caught a glimpse of her twice on the second day we were here and reminded them of what I said when we were at the ice cream parlor, about someone following me.

"There are several huge concerns," Mom said, "The idea

that anyone could be mean to a child. That is not acceptable! And ... the fact that Mattie's grandmother was denied access to see her family on the outside."

Jessica leaned forward and whispered. "And where's her grandmother now? Did they kill her?"

Mom jumped back in her chair with that statement. "Let's not even think like that, girls. This could all be a misunderstanding. Now I don't mean that in a bad way—I just mean that could be the way Mattie perceived things."

Since I was the one who had the actual conversation with Mattie, I knew better. This girl might be a little sneaky and even a little paranoid, but her perception seemed pretty good to me. I kept that to myself, hoping Mattie would convince them herself in the near future.

Chapter Twelve
Secret Night Mission

SUNDAY WAS A day of rest for most, and we had fallen into that grouping. The upstairs wall had shelves lined with more books than we could read in a lifetime, and a two-foot space was filled with games at the end of each row. The girls were playing dominoes on a downstairs table nestled in the bay window. I found a book about a dog named Lassie, and even with the stress I was under, I found it captivating. Lassie had been accidently left behind when his family moved. He crossed miles and miles of rough terrain to find them. Everywhere he stopped to take a rest someone helped him, but then tried to keep him. He always found a way to get back on the trail to find his family. I somehow could see Mattie in that dog. She wanted no part of any normal life until she found her grandma. I put the bookmark in place and ran down the stairs, my mind brimming with thoughts.

"Mom! I remembered something important!" I slid across the kitchen in my socks landing perfectly in front of her. She put up her hands to catch me in case I slid too far.

"What?" she exclaimed.

"Mattie said her uncle was a police officer and she came with her grandma eight years ago!"

Mom's eyes widened as she tried to comprehend what I was insinuating, "You think she's Matt's niece?"

Mom exploded inside, not even waiting for my answer, "That would be terrible Joey!"

She paced the floor, looking down, with her hands on her hips before speaking, "But the scenario and time line certainly fit exactly what Matt told us. And Sturgis! He was awful nervous when I asked him about a Ruthie . . . The fact he's gone now, makes me worry. I hope I didn't put all of us in danger. Darn I should have kept my mouth shut!"

My brain was in high gear as Mom ranted, I was trying to remember any similarity between Matt and Mattie. "Mattie kinda looks like Matt and she's got big dimples just like him!" I moved to look into Mom's face, "When can I go talk to her again?"

"Let me think about that, Joey," she answered.

I went back to my book and had a hard time concentrating. *If Officer Darden's mom and niece were in trouble, he would want to know!*

Mom decided we would go find Mattie, that night. "I don't think you can fit through the chain on the gate," I said.

She thought about it, then responded, "We will cross that bridge when we get to it."

After dinner, she sat the girls down and told them the plan. They hated it. Cassandra brought up a very good point. "If they catch Joey they will just consider him being curious. If they catch you, Mom? Big trouble!"

Mom agreed it would be impossible to explain. She

wouldn't go inside the park; she would wait outside, hidden. We all came to terms with that plan. It was dark by eight, but we would wait thirty minutes after the bell rang before we left. We used our time to find dark clothing, which was impossible. We settled on a dark blue sheet-set we'd found. We wrapped our bodies up and ran as fast as we could, following between the houses on a mapped route Mom had composed. All went well and Mom found a spot behind a bush close to the gate. I went through the gate, realizing the chain wasn't tight at all, but decided not to tell her. I kept going. My plan was to check out the Barbie house first, but I heard the familiar whistle. I looked to the bumper cars and saw Mattie standing below the bumper-car platform. She smiled as the light she was holding made her face glow.

What I saw next felt like a dream. I opened and closed my eyes to clear the blur. A light popped on behind her, glowing down across the area. I recoiled as I saw the same muscular man who had her cornered on the sidewalk. In the bright light he looked like the giant from *Jack and the Beanstalk*. He was huge, with arms bigger than most men's legs. His hair was long and the wind was tossing it into his face as he jerked Mattie up by the back of her collar. She was caught by surprise and screamed at the top of her lungs. Her body bounced to and fro, like a rag doll dancing in midair; I wondered if she was doing it to escape or was he shaking her senseless. He held her up like a trophy he was proudly displaying. She scratched and clawed like a cat who had gone crazy. The screaming was as sharp as a knife and it pierced right through my very soul. My whole system revolted. I literally felt my body stiffening up, starting at my feet, then gradually working its way up. Unable to move, I felt my throat tightened. That was when I blacked out...

When I awoke, my head hurt and Mom was holding me. The dark blue sheet was wrapped tightly around both of us. The best I could tell as I tried to see in the dark was that we were in the Barbie playhouse. "Shhhh." Mom put her finger over my lips to keep me quiet. No need; I didn't have the strength to make a sound. Mom cradled me, motionless in the dark. I fell asleep until a glimmer of light shined in. Mom had cracked open the playhouse door and was rambling to herself, saying she thought it was close to six o'clock. After observing to be sure no one was there, we went to the last place I had seen Mattie. Her small light was lying beside the bumper-car entrance. We followed a path to the pavilion. The fence had been cut and there was a pile of cigarette butts close by. He had been waiting for her. We crawled through the opening and looked, but she was gone.

The walk back to our cottage was bleak and quiet. Cassandra, Jessica, and Jody were asleep in the floor, close to the front door. Mom woke them and put all four of us in her bed. She sat in the chair beside us.

A knock at the door woke me up. My body shook as I peered through the crack of Mom's partially open bedroom door. Mom opened the front door, to see who was knocking. It was one of our morning class teachers checking on us to make sure everything was okay. I looked at the clock and was surprised it was noon. The girls stood beside me and when I pointed to the clock, their eyes enlarged, shocked we'd all slept so far past school time.

We heard Mom speaking. "We've been up all night with

a stomach bug. The girls are in bed, but they'll be there tomorrow." The four of us tiptoed back to the bed, in case the teacher came in to see. Before the teacher left, I heard her tell Mom that she needed to check in with Miss Barrett about her job assignment.

"Be prepared to start tomorrow," the teacher said. "Just follow the girls at eight and you will see the other women going to the manufacturing unit. That's where you're scheduled to work from 8:15 to 4:15."

Mom's voice sounded subdued as she said, "Okay." Moments later, she crawled into bed with us and told Cassandra and the twins what had happened last night. I questioned how she knew all the details. She revealed that she had not stayed outside the gate but had followed me and saw the man kidnap Mattie. She picked me up after I'd collapsed and took us into the Barbie playhouse. I held Mom's hand, so grateful that she'd been there. She smiled at me. After a long question-and-answer session, we lay in the bed, each of us lost in our own thoughts. I didn't know if Mattie was okay. Was she and her grandma being held, or were they both gone from the park?

Mom's half-lie to the teacher came to pass. We all had stomach trouble the rest of the day. Mom thought it was caused from our action-packed night, because none of us had eaten anything since yesterday. Around four, I found the motivation to get up and shower. I put on my required clothes and went outside. I didn't know what I was looking for—yes, I did, and I was hoping to see Mattie scurrying about to find her next safe place. I was shocked to see men working inside the park. Except for Sturgis and that Hulk of a man I'd seen twice, (last night and on the sidewalk the day Miss Barrett almost caught Mattie) I had never seen men inside the women's home. They were fixing the fence and put a new gate on the park entrance with no chain. I stopped to talk with them and was told they were not allowed to talk to the girls. On my way back to our cottage, I had a notion that those men surely didn't come through the rollercoaster wall like we did. I would watch and see if there was another way for the workers to come and go. I cut back through the neighborhood to see which way they were going and followed behind. They trudged back up the mountain. I was disappointed to see they were leaving the same way we had come in. It was too far to see much else, but I did see the door open in the same spot it opened for us. I guessed I learned one thing: the door could be opened from this side also. I made my way up and down each row of cottages from north to south. I knew in my heart I wouldn't see her even if she had escaped, she's an expert at hiding.

Chapter Thirteen
Surprise Visitor

WHEN I OPENED the door, I could smell food cooking. I was anxious to let Mom and the girls in on what I had learned, because I knew they were as vested in this little red haired girl as much as I was now. Something had changed . . . I wasn't sure what had happened while I was gone, but everyone was dressed and the last-day-on-death-row mood was gone. Mom was talking loud and festive as if she was auditioning for an acting role. When she saw me, she ran to hug me like she hadn't seen me for days.

"Cassandra!" she called. "Come stir the macaroni for me."

I watched as Cassandra immediately obeyed, which was not at all typical, she usually complained for a moment while she presented the case, it was my turn to take the job. I was suspicious; something more was going on in our cottage. Mom whispered in my ear, "Go up to your bathroom." Then she said aloud, "Go up and change, sweetie! I will be up to get your laundry in just a minute!"

That was the final absurdity. I knew Mom well enough to know she wasn't acting normal. I stood with my hands on my hips, ready to delve into it, when Mom winked and said, "Go on upstairs, honey."

Not understanding any of it, I did what she said with no question. I moved slowly, watching for any hints as to what was up. Mom reached the top of the stairs while I was still on the landing. She took my arm and walked me into the bathroom. I turned around, ready to question Mom, when I saw her. Mattie was wrapped up in a towel, positioned on the edge of the tub. My eyes had to do a double take to make sure it was real. I immediately rushed over and hugged her, almost pushing her into the waiting hot water. The joy that filled my heart brought tears; it was as if someone had given me a new bike after mine had been run over.

Mom shut the door. "Mattie was in my closet this morning. I went in to get dressed and found her sleeping in the corner."

"How did you get away?" I asked ecstatically.

She stood up, holding the towel tightly around her body, trying to think of the short answer. I looked her over. Her face and neck had scratches, most likely where that giant man had tried to keep his grasp on her. "I flipped and flopped until I could get a good bite in on him.

He finally let me go after I drew blood. He roared at me, 'you viper! All the money in the world ain't worth this'!" Her animation told me she was complimented by his assessment. "I ran as fast as I could and hid in your trashcan for a while, then I climbed the trellis and found my way to your mom's closet." I could see Mom had gained her trust with the revelation, that we knew her uncle Matt. That made me happy, knowing I was right about Matt Darden being her uncle.

These new surroundings certainly brought out a much softer side to Mattie compared to the wild animal side I had previously seen. She looked at Mom and then back to me sharing the plan, "Your mom's gonna help me find my grandma."

Mom nodded and put her arm around her. "You'll be safe here until we come up with a plan to find out what happened to your grandmother. In the meantime, Mattie's gonna keep a low profile." Mattie agreed as Mom continued, "Mattie said a lot of the cottages have cameras, which is why she will stay up here in the bathroom until we know for sure if this cottage has a camera."

We ate dinner upstairs and brainstormed on what to do next. Dinner turned out to be quite an event. Watching Mattie eat a home-cooked meal—the first one since she'd run away—was epic for us. She didn't wolf it down like I would have. She ate one small bite at a time, savoring each piece of macaroni. Mom had helped her bathe around her injuries and her matted red hair was clean, plump, and curly. As I was admiring how pretty Mattie was, Mom caught me looking and raised her eyebrows.

"We do have one secret we need to tell you, Mattie, and I think we all agree from this point on that all secrets need to be brought out into the open." We all agreed. "You may be wondering why we moved here," Mom said.

Mattie thought about it before she answered, "You must have been in danger?"

"Yes, I was, as a matter of fact." Mom showed Mattie some of the bruising she still had from earlier that week. "We all needed a safe place away from the man who did this. Your uncle Matt knew about this place . . ."

Mattie's face turned sad, "My grandma wondered why he didn't ever come back to check on us."

"They wouldn't let him," I bellowed. "They forbid him to go any farther than the front gate of the big amusement park."

Mattie looked disheartened. "Grandma missed him so bad."

Mom spoke up, "Mattie someone was telling him you were both very happy and wanted to stay. Most likely so he wouldn't get concerned about why you hadn't contacted him."

We were all so emotionally charged, Mom didn't get to her original point, which was that I wasn't really a girl. The bell would ring soon, so we turned the kitchen light off and Mom hoisted me up to the very top of the cabinets with a flashlight. I crawled the full length and couldn't find a camera. Not even a pinhole where one could be hidden. Our plan was to search every inch of the house. My designated area was the kitchen and living zone. After searching along the walls and inspecting each brick, I crawled inside the fireplace, wondering if a camera could be hanging down and angled to see into the living and kitchen area. I made a very strange discovery. Beyond the firebox, to the right and to the left, it was open, and it extended the full length behind the brick walls. I ran to get the others, explaining what I had found.

"Just beyond the firebox are two open area's." Demonstrating, I crawled through the fireplace opening again and stood behind the wall.

"That's crazy, I wonder why they did that." Mom said as

she poked her head in to investigate.

"The older houses have recessed bookshelves built into both sides of the fireplace," Mattie said.

Jody and Jessica climbed inside. "Wow, this is a great hiding place."

The bell sounded and the lights flickered three times. Mom spoke fast, "Mattie, you sleep in Joy's bed, and Joy will sleep with me." We moved fast and within sixty seconds, we were all in our assigned sleeping quarters.

I always did a lot of kicking in my sleep, or so I have been told. So I fully expected Mom to complain about it and move me to the couch. "No, you did fine, honey." I'd slept like a log and never woke once but had my doubts about not kicking, because I was all twisted in the top sheet when I got up. Mom's piece of mind—knowing I was safe—was more important to her. She was dressed in her khaki blouse and skirt, and her hair was pulled up in a ponytail. Mom's hair was even darker than mine and the girls, and when we could afford it she went to the beauty shop to perm it. The perm was gone and a slight frizz had taken over. She had already eaten, but fixed eggs and toast with orange juice for us (the orange juice was a treat to Mattie).

Mattie and I were the only ones left at the table, and I had made up my mind about something I wanted to tell her privately. I kept glancing over and finally said, "I want to tell you something between me and you."

She scowled. "I already know you're a boy. The girls told me your secret last night."

"No, not that." I cringed a little from embarrassment. "I'm not sure when, but if I get the chance, I'm gonna stay inside the school building to look around." She stared at me closely, sizing me up, no doubt wondering if I had what it took to do that. I continued, "If I'm late, or don't get back, tell Mom what I did."

Mom walked in talking to Cassandra, and Mattie discreetly affirmed to me she would handle it. Mom was loading down the right-side opening behind the fireplace wall with pillows, books, and a packed lunch for Mattie. "I won't worry so much if I know you have a safe place, Mattie," Mom said.

Mattie assured her she thought it was best and would be careful not to be seen. It was 7:45; I finished dressing and stood by the door with Mom and the girls till the bell rang. Mattie had already settled into her safe place.

Chapter Fourteen

Mandatory Search

WE RUSHED TO join a large group approaching the sidewalk that ended at the school doorway. I looked at Mom, knowing something was wrong. The crowd was enormous compared to Friday. A large platform had been placed in the center of the large field that butted to the foot of the mountain. A speaker system was on the ground and a large podium with a microphone was centered in front of several teachers. Miss Barrett was tapping the head of the microphone to test it; the sound was loud enough that people were covering their ears.

Miss Barrett spoke into the microphone. "Yesterday, Miss Clarkson came to every door to make sure all would be here today. I appreciate that you came promptly."

"Like we had a choice," I muttered under my breath.

"For over sixteen years, we have run a very successful women and girls' home, and except for a few small things, all has gone well. As most of you have noticed, we changed what we call our 'doorkeeper' position. We are sad to say that Sturgis decided to leave. I will be taking over that position and you will find that I am a little less, let's just say ... a little less tolerable."

I looked around the crowd, but no one showed the least bit of negativity with the controlling way she spoke. In fact, not a word was spoken.

Miss Barrett bellowed on. "Our rules are few and simple, and I expect cooperation from every resident, children and adults alike. With that being said, we have a child on the loose in this park who has kept this place turned upside down for several months now. Her name is Matilda Watson and she is ten years old. She was last seen in filthy, dirty khaki's and a large mass of frizzy red hair. She is dangerous and has injured one of our security guards."

I clung to Mom's skirt, as I was feeling light-headed. Cassandra, who had sworn off nail biting, had just taken it back up. Jody and Jessica fearfully scanned Mom's face.

"Every square inch of this park will be searched today while you are at school and work. If you have seen or know where she is, speak up now." Miss Barrett waited a full minute for a response. "If she is found on your premises and we find out you knew but didn't tell us, you will be punished." She patiently waited for any response. "So be it. Follow your normal routine for the day. All the searching will be halted at four-o'clock. You can go to your homes after work or school."

Mom's hand was sweating as I grabbed it. "She will be fine, girls. You just go to class and have a nice day." Her demeanor showed anxiety, but she clearly had no intentions of worrying us. We had seen Mom stressed before, and I could tell she was scared for Mattie and maybe a little for all of us.

I might have misread my interpretation of the crowd,

because a low-level negative chatter could be heard. Clearly the children were affected by Miss Barrett's overbearing speech. Word had gotten back to her and she came to our class to speak. Miss Barrett said she wanted to reassure us that all was well. Softening up her harsh tone, she came across as way too mushy and contrived. This gal was a spin doctor, manipulator deluxe, and I knew she had other things aside from our well-being on her mind. But she was good; her speech changed the atmosphere among the girls drastically. I think the clincher was the ice-cream coupons she told the teacher to pass out at the end of the day. I was pretty sure that was a last minute buy-out. She might be calculated but also pretty clever.

The day dragged on forever, and I had totally revised my mental day planner. The memo to investigate for clues after-hours was completely scrapped. I would get home to Mattie as fast as my legs would carry me, convincing myself with all my heart that she would still be there. With Miss Barrett's words about being punished replaying in my head, I had a mental picture of that big brute who'd attacked Mattie at the amusement park dragging all of us out to the public square and stringing us up. That was as far as I would let that daydream play out before I shook myself back to reality.

I watched the clock count down to the last second, but I still jumped when the bell went off. I was convinced, as I looked up at that round scrap of green metal in passing, that all the bells, including the one at our cottage, were really fire alarms. The intensity, the dulcimers, the panic that ensued when ringing began. Everything about them threw the human spirit into unease. I got in line to leave. Cassandra and the twins squeezed in behind me. There was no running allowed on the sidewalk. We impatiently followed, passing when possible, then running as fast as I could when I got out in the open. Not a person was out and about. The searching must have been completed, even though it was only three o'clock.

I stopped on the porch and paced for a moment to calm my anxiety. I opened the door to quietness and listened closely as I looked around. I didn't go straight to the fireplace, and thank goodness I didn't call out to her, because one minute later two women from a search team came down the stairs. I saw the girls coming to the porch, so I opened the door and stepped out. "We gotta stay out here until they get done," I said in a curious tone. My sisters looked inside before following my order. Of course, I believed it had all been a ploy to see if we would run in and see if "she" was still safe and sound.

The two women excused themselves and crossed through the cottages to the next sidewalk, a street over. Apparently, someone had suspicions we were involved. We sat on the couch in silence until we saw Mom ambling down the sidewalk. We all bolted outside to greet her.

"They were here when Joey got home," Cassandra said. I sighed deeply and told her how it had gone down.

"Good, Joey. You did well. I'm pretty sure I would have ran straight to the fireplace."

"Me too," Cassandra said, and the twins agreed.

Mom peeked in the fireplace, but not until we did a thorough search of the downstairs just in case they had planted cameras while we were gone. "She's sound asleep," Mom whispered through a smile. We all moved to the kitchen, relieved beyond belief. Mom reached across the counter for all of our hands. "Somehow we will all get through this," she said as she patted our hands.

"One of us needs to break out and bring back the police," Jessica reasoned. I was surprised to hear her words, but knew that was about the only chance we had. Even if Mattie's grandma was found, they weren't going to let us leave. We let Mattie sleep while Mom cooked dinner. The cottage smelled of leftover fried chicken. While the chicken was heating up, she made more macaroni and cheese with a green salad. This was the most days in a row we had ever had macaroni and cheese. The girls set the table for dinner, upstairs, just because it felt safer. I kept my eye on the fireplace.

"Can I wake her, Mom?" I asked.

"Sure, sweetie, go ahead, but check out front to make sure all is safe first."

I sat on the swing and watched up and down the sidewalk for a few moments. No one was out. "Coast is clear," I said, saluting as I came through the screen door, then pushing shut the main door. Jody beat me to the fireplace and was climbing through to wake Mattie.

"Darn!" I accidently said, which drew a scowl from Mom. Mattie looked like a freshly hatched critter, stretching and rubbing her eyes. "Did you sleep the whole day?" I asked.

"I guess so," she mumbled. "I did clean up the dishes first!" She pointed to the sink.

Cassandra, who appreciated that because it was her turn to do the dishes, said, "Thank you, Mattie!"

We gave Mattie a few minutes to freshen up, then gathered around the upstairs table. Mom reiterated Miss Barrett's burning speech from that morning.

"I knew I was high priority, but to hold an assembly to discuss catching me?" Mattie was in awe thinking about it, then her expression turned sad. "I don't want you guys to get in trouble protecting me. As soon as I can find a safe place, I will go."

"Not happening." Mom asserted her motherly authority in a normal tone, then said it louder to make sure Mattie understood. "Not happening, so don't even try." Mom's scowling face proved that she meant what she said.

"Promise us," I threw in for good measure, even though I knew Mom had covered it.

"I promise," Mattie said, putting her hand in the air as if she were under oath. Mom sat on the porch to keep watch while we did the dishes, then went up to play Monopoly. Between rolls of the dice, I asked Mattie things I needed to know.

"Where exactly have you looked for your grandma?"

"Well, I knew they took her toward Berryhill Mountain because I watched them. When I was able to get in the school, I looked around in the areas that weren't locked. I even checked in Mr. Berryhill's office—they don't keep it locked, you know." I was surprised by that.

"Have you seen anyone come or go by any other entrance than through the rollercoaster?" I asked.

"Mmm . . . not really," she said thoughtfully. "But one thing I have considered: all the big things they have in here you can't get it through that little opening."

She was right; there must be another opening and I was going to find it.

Chapter Fifteen
Follow the Bunny

WE ALL AGREED that Mattie should sleep in her safe place to be on the safe side. There was no way to know for sure if they had singled us out to be here when we got home from school or if it was just a coincidence. But the thought of them barreling through the door in the middle of the night was not far-fetched. We would stay prepared.

We awoke with no nighttime drama, thank goodness. The kitchen table seemed to be our "war room," and as I approached the table, I realized Mom had not said a word about how her new job placement had worked out. I asked her and listened as she skirted around a full answer with small chitchat about it not being so bad.

Mattie in her usual blunt manner spoke, "My grandma said it was horrible."

Mom agreed, "Something about the whole thing doesn't make sense. There are women working with us who I don't think live here. Lots of Asian ladies, old and young. The oldest women seem to be struggling. I am new, so they put me in packaging. That's where you vacuum seal all the packages shut and decide which bin it goes in to be shipped. In the afternoon, I went to a special training class for all the other departments. I guess whichever one I'm good at, that's where I will move in six weeks. I can see right now the steaming department is the most hated. A few of those ladies looked like they were ready to pass out long before their shift ended. Most of those gals are older, and I guess it also has an evening shift, because a new group was coming in when we left."

Mattie was visibly shaken. "That's where my grandma worked the last week before they took her. She would be so tired, and if they didn't have all their work done, they were punished."

"How?" I asked.

"They had to stay and finish, even if it took the whole night."

"What do they steam?" Cassandra asked.

"Animal hides," Mom answered. "The hides are used for purses, jackets, belts, et cetera. I heard one supervisor scolding one of the steamers because she could still see the lice running around."

Mattie nodded her head. "My grandma and I got lice." Mattie scratched her head.

"I wondered why there was such a large bottle of lice shampoo in with the other shampoos," Jody said.

Jessica scrunched her nose. "That's gross!"

Mom looked at the clock as she handed Mattie her lunch sack, then kissed all of us on the forehead. "Try to have a good day, kids. This will all work out—you will see!" She was clearly trying to encourage us, and I sure wanted to believe her.

No more searches came to the cottage that week, and there was no significant progress on finding Mattie's grandma. There was just no time to make any big moves, with school and the curfew. Mom's job was taking a toll on her. Cassandra took over the cooking, and the rest of us did all the clean-up. When the weekend came, Mattie insisted we go to the amusement park, as she would be fine at home alone. Mom wouldn't hear of it, and that was when she brought forth an idea she had been mulling over. She'd found some black shoe polish and doused Mattie's trimmed hair with it. She let it dry naturally, then sealed it in with the hairdryer. "Viola!" Mom said, you look like one of us. Cassandra went to the park entrance to check things out and found that the gate watcher was just a teenager. Mom felt sure she wouldn't notice if we entered with others.

When we arrived at the sidewalk closest to the entrance, we waited for a group and blended in with several families entering together. Mom patrolled while we had fun. We had a signal—she would scream and faint in the midway if she saw Miss Barrett or any of her assigned assistants searching the park. In the center of the park were benches and picnic tables scattered around a scenic pond with a large fountain. We could see Mom from any ride, although we avoided several, including the bumper cars. It was a nice break from the stress we had experienced the past week. We got our ice-cream coupons and the ice cream to go, eating it on the way home. We trusted Gilda, but there was no reason to get her involved, Mom decided.

Mom was not herself, mentally or physically. She retired to her room after falling asleep on the couch. It was still early afternoon; the girls played Monopoly upstairs, and I sat on the porch with a book, *Treasure Island* by Robert Louis Stevenson, which was the only book other than *Lassie* that wasn't totally written for girls. I loved it, but my focus on the book had a competitor: Berryhill Mountain. I had never been past the school entrance and certainly had not walked around to the backside. I laid the book down and started walking. I knew it would be a fifty-fifty chance to completely make it, not only to my destination, but back from this exploration. I was prepared. It was worth it to me. After all, it had been a full week of no progress finding Mattie's grandma. The only thing progressing was Mom's daily exhaustion.

I kept my head down and moved fairly slow. I had decided if I was questioned, I would lie and say I was following a bunny's trail. It sounded logical to me. What was really funny, after crawling a little ways, I noticed tiny little feet had left impressions in the powdery soft dirt. I scanned up ahead to discover a small bunny was hopping (the high concentration of tracks told me it frequented this way quite often). Dismayed I was on its trail, the bunny stepped up its speed. I followed it around the mountainside. Once I was under the strip of windows, I decided to let my back recover and maybe even peek inside. I noticed the bunny continuing on and decided I would follow it to the corner first, to see where it was going. It disappeared into a row of bushes that lined the back edge of the mountain. I crawled back and peeked into the classroom. Several women were picking up the rows of hanging fabric that Cassandra and her group had ironed this week. The window was cracked and I put my ear up to hear.

"This is not enough! We need twice this amount, and

these still have to be sewn and packaged." I didn't recognize the person talking, but she was talking to Miss Clarkson, one of the afternoon teachers.

"Don't worry, I will make sure it gets done before Monday," Miss Clarkson assured her.

Sure sounded like a quota had to be met. The idea that they were just training and teaching flew out the window with their voices.

Chapter Sixteen
Eavesdropping Gold Mine

AFTER A MINUTE of ear-straining silence, I got back on my knees to continue. I wanted to see if the bunny had a home in the bushes. After only a few feet of progress, I heard someone yell, "Damn!" Turning back, I lifted my ear to the window. The voice sounded like Miss Barrett's, and she said it again. She was mad and chomping on someone verbally.

"Clarkson, you get this fabric to the shop and get those women to work! How many do we have under detainment? And don't just count those who are able to work!"

"Uh . . . only six or seven," Miss Clarkson said hesitantly. "Ruthie has been pretty sick though."

"Well, you get 'em working on this order right now, including little Miss Ruthie! You get that order finished or I will have their heads on a platter!"

"Ma'am," Miss Clarkson said meekly. "Ruthie needs the doctor."

"What doctor? You heard the man as plain as me—he quit! He ain't coming back! You go through all that stuff he left and find her something—she will be just fine!"

I heard Miss Clarkson run across the room, then Miss Barrett yelled, continuing with the same ugly tone, "You let Sturgis out and send him up here! He can move all this fabric down to the shop! And you tell him he better behave or I won't give Ruthie any medicine!" Miss Barrett stomped across the room and left.

Oh, for joy, for joy ... I was elated to hear Sturgis was still here and Mattie's grandma Ruth Anne was alive, but flabbergasted to think they were holding her and Sturgis against their will. My brain was racing ninety miles an hour. I had to make a decision: Did I go back and tell Mom, Mattie, and the girls what I had heard, or did I keep moving and find a way out to bring back help? As I hashed it all out in my brain, the pros and cons both made sense. The relief of knowing Ruth Anne was alive could be monumental in relieving everyone's stress, especially Mattie's. And the fact, as far as we knew, that they hadn't killed anyone yet was encouraging. Mom would be absolutely blown away to hear Sturgis wasn't in on all this. He was a prisoner! I wished Mom were here so I could let her make the decision, but then I thought better of it—she would tell me to come back to the cottage. That would be a mistake. Who would go for help? I wouldn't want her or any of the girls trying to navigate this mountainous terrain. I knew I could do it.

I could hear the sound of coat hangers being slid across the large metal bars they had been stored on. I peeked in and was surprised—not at who it was, but at his condition. It was Sturgis looking completely worse for wear. The finely dressed, no-hair-out-of-place refined gentleman we'd met on our first day here was barely recognizable. I scanned him up and down for injuries; his bloodied lip was swollen to double its normal size, he had a black eye, and he was limping. There were homemade bandages on both of his knees. As he loaded his arms with the fabrics, I heard a metal rumbling noise that was gradually getting louder. Something large was coming down the hallway. I ducked to listen.

"Sturgis, use this cart for the fabric, it'll make it easier." It was Miss Clarkson. "I'm taking this medicine down to Ruthie right now; I found some antibiotics in the doctor's storage closet."

"Thank you, Miss. Clarkson," Sturgis said politely. "When all this gets brought out into the open, I will make sure they go easy on you."

I didn't hear her reply, and after a moment, thinking she had left, I lifted myself to eye level to look in. She was leaning against the doorjamb, trying to pull herself together. She wiped her face with her arm and closed the door as she left. This could be my chance. I tapped on the window until Sturgis looked my way. He pulled the rack of clothes to block me from view. He lifted the window a teeny bit and *wham!* It slammed shut and an ear-piercing alarm forced me flat on the ground. Miss Barrett was yelling. Even with the alarm, her profuse cursing was easily distinguishable. Moving frantically to reach the corner, I hoped to turn before she opened the window to look out. My fear wasn't for myself; I was sure Sturgis was getting punished for my actions. I crawled as fast as I could ... crawling inside the bushes and strategically turning myself around, so I could see those approaching from the south. I lay there and watched until dark, then decided I needed to go back and tell Mom.

Moving through the darkness, close to the mountain's edge, my destination was the southwest corner, I wanted to make a mad dash from there. I looked up and saw a floodlight mounted on a corner ledge about fifteen feet up. I rolled over and saw rows of floodlights all the way around the ledge that followed the perimeter. I felt relieved I hadn't caused enough motion to set any of them off. I lay there until it was light enough to take the floodlight motion detectors off my problem list but still dark enough to get home undetected.

I ran across the openness of the yard, staying off the sidewalk that led to the school. I ran from cover to cover until I reached my street. I heard a faint whistle and saw Mattie squatting in the bushes surrounding the last house on the street. I followed her to our back patio and climbed up the trellis. Mom was waiting with the door open. The girls were standing beside her.

Mom pulled Mattie up first, thanking her, which told me she had been worried enough to let Mattie go out looking for me. By the time she pulled me up, she was crying. She escorted us inside.

"You scared me to death, Joey."

"I'm sorry, Mom. I got trapped and couldn't get back home without being seen. I was gonna wait until dark, but then I saw the motion-detection floodlights and had to wait until almost daylight."

She hugged me tight. "Don't scare me like that again!" she scolded.

"Mom, I saw Sturgis."

She looked at me with severe reservations. "What do you mean you saw him? Did you speak with him?"

"No... well, I tapped on the window. He's on our side, Mom! He moved a rack of fabric to hide me from view."

Her expression perked up. "Did he say anything to you?"

"No, he didn't have a chance." I got teary eyed. "After I tapped on the window, he tried to raise it so he could talk with me and a very loud alarm went off."

Cassandra reached her hand to Mom. "We heard it all the way here, didn't we Mom?"

Mom nodded as she spoke, "That's when we discovered you missing. We thought you were the one that set that alarm off and they had you in custody."

I groaned, feeling bad I had caused Mom so much distress. "Well, I was okay, but poor Sturgis took the brunt of it. He looked so bad, like someone had beat him up, and when that alarm went off... oh my goodness, I thought sure Miss Barrett was gonna knock his head off. She was yelling so loud, I could hear her through the window, even with that alarm blaring."

Everyone started speaking at once, but I put up my hand, "I got news about Mattie's grandma." I turned to Mattie. "Your grandma is okay, they have her under detainment." I said it slowly, hoping it wouldn't overwhelm her all at once.

Mattie's shoulders crumpled in relief at my words, but her face was frantic as she spoke, "How did she look? Did you talk to her?"

"No, I didn't see her, but I heard Miss Clarkson talking about her. She called her 'Ruthie.'"

Mattie nodded. "Yes, that's what everyone here called her."

"Don't get worried, because I don't think it's really bad,

but Miss Clarkson said she was sick. I think Miss Clarkson likes your grandma, because she told Miss Barrett she was too sick to work and she found her some medicine." I turned to Mom. "The doctor told Miss Barrett he's not coming back."

Mom's face furrowed up. "That's not good, especially if Mattie's grandma is sick. Did they say why he's not coming back? Did you get the impression the doctor knew of the criminal things going on here?"

"Yes. That's exactly how Miss Barrett stated it—like he knew and wanted nothing more to do with this place."

"Let's hope and pray if the doctor feels that way he will tell someone and get Ruth Anne some help."

I told them everything I had heard and seen, including the big order that must be ready by Monday. "Mom, Mattie's grandma was right: They are under pressure to keep all these women working to fulfill all the clothes orders. That's why they don't want anyone to leave. I heard Miss Clarkson say they have six or seven people detained!"

"Oh my lord! That's just insane! Who do they think they are... some kind of prison system?" She put her hands on her hips and spoke with rebellion, "Well, I got some bad news for whoever is running this show. There is no chance this could ever be a long-term, workable plan!" I smiled, feeling so proud of my mother. She was displaying a new spunk I'd never seen. She certainly didn't display any of this confidence at the duplex, under my stepdads control.

Jody and Jessica had bowls of cereal ready when we came downstairs. As soon as we sat down, we heard a knock at the door. Mattie tiptoed to her spot behind the brick wall and we hid her bowl in the sink. Mom answered the door while we listened. It was Miss Clarkson.

"Hello, Mrs. Randal, I'm sorry to interrupt your Sunday." She was speaking very sugary, sweet polite. "Miss Barrett is requiring all the women to come back in to work for a few hours today. Please be at the platform promptly at nine."

Mom nodded and stepped back inside. "Well, that confirms some of what you said, Joey. They are under some stress to meet that deadline." She turned to look at Mattie, "And to be honest, I would prefer all of us women to go back in. Then maybe they will let your grandma rest." We all agreed.

Chapter Seventeen
Overtime, Overload

MOM SAID WE could go to the park, but gave the girls clear instruction that under no circumstances was I to be out of their sight. I could understand that. Mattie had a new glow about her and had come to like her hair dark. The black shoe polish was a bit messy, but it made her look like she belonged in our family. We stayed away from the center of the amusement park and sat at a table on the far side of the pond. It sat up high and was partially covered. We had a bird's-eye view of most of the park. The park was quiet since all the moms were working. A few of the older girls were having a good time spinning in circles in the bumper-car arena. The twins and I had a very competitive rock-skimming contest going until we saw the "No rock throwing" sign. Mattie and Cassandra were coaxing the geese up to the picnic table with a piece of cake they'd found in the trash. I loved this place—we all did. If not for the bad stuff, like Miss Barrett, it would be the perfect community to raise children.

We got our ice-cream coupon and sat up at the soda fountain bar, completely forgetting about the need to keep

Mattie secret. Gilda handed each of us a chocolate cone, and when she got to Mattie, she winked at her. "I'm glad to see you doing so well," she said under her breath, barely moving her mouth. I had always felt like Gilda was "one of us," but we really couldn't take the chance of talking to her about it. Even now, there was no way to know for sure whether she would, under pressure, turn us in.

"We should probably go," Cassandra said. I could tell she had thought better of our being here.

Gilda touched Cassandra's hand and whispered, "This secret is safe with me."

"Thank you," Cassandra whispered.

We all filed out the door and walked fairly fast. Cassandra was holding the twins' hands as she led the way. "I don't think Gilda will tell," I told Mattie.

"I don't think she will either," Mattie replied.

We stayed home the rest of the day, a little on edge. Cassandra kept watch on the porch, as she read *Treasure Island* (she had started reading it while I was gone yesterday). She had set up a sign for trouble—rapping three times hard on the glass window. Dusk came and went, and Cassandra and Mattie fixed dinner (soup and grilled cheese). I wasn't good at waiting, so now I was out on the porch extremely worried. It was dark and had been for hours. Cassandra had all of us take our bath and get our pajamas on, then insisted we all go to bed. I fell asleep in Mom's bed and heard her come in slightly before daybreak. She fell into bed with a groan. She pulled her pillow close into her arms and fell asleep, whispering, "Goodnight, Joey."

We let Mom sleep, but only after a ten-minute discussion on whether we should wake her. She was awake before we left and came into the kitchen as we were perched at the door, waiting for the bell to ring. She kissed all of us. "I go in at noon. I will see you tonight!" She raised her voice to compete with the ringing bell.

I was surprised they were again having the girls stop at the platform. Some grumbled, but I was anxious to hear what they had to say. It was just Miss. Clarkson today. "Hello, girls!" She started with that sickening, sweet tone again. "I apologize for the late hour your mothers arrived home, and I want to explain. It takes a lot of money to keep all of this up and running." She used her arms to encircle the area around us. "The only source of income we have is the clothing line that we make and sell to our vendors. Your mothers will be working late the rest of this month because of today's missed deadline."

Da$!?!%?!, I thought, shocked I had such words in my vocabulary! Much to my sisters' dismay, I raised my hand and furiously waved it in the air, realizing that I didn't even care if I was crossing the line.

"Don't do it, Joey!" Jody cautioned.

"You better be using your best girl voice!" Jessica whispered as she pinched my upper arm. It must have seemed out of the ordinary for someone to speak up, every head was turned, looking at me. I had caught Miss Clarkson off guard; she looked a little stunned as she pointed for me to speak.

"My mom didn't get home till almost daylight. How did they miss the deadline?" I shouted with a tinge of attitude.

She nodded. "I appreciate your question. Your name is Randal, isn't it?" I figured Mom had told them our name was the same as hers, so I nodded. "What's your first name?" She was drawing this out longer than I had planned.

"Joy!" I yelled as soprano as I could.

"Okay, well, Joy, I was told a lot of the fabric that was cut, ironed, and ready to be sewn had been damaged in some way. We had to order in new fabric. The ladies spent most of last evening preparing the fabric and were only able to construct about half of the garments. And now they must finish the rest."

By now, the soupy-sweet way she spoke to me as she stood on that stage, all bent over with her hands clasped like she was talking to a two-year-old, just made me livid! "That's not right," I mumbled, but in a normal level talking voice.

"I'm sorry, but what did you say?" she asked.

Cassandra answered, "He said, 'you're right'!" as she kicked me in the shin.

"Okay, well, thank you for your question, Joy, and thank you all again for understanding. You are free to go to your classes."

Chapter Eighteen
Time to Make a Move

I STOMPED FAR away from my sisters and stood in the crowd waiting for the door to open. I spotted an opening that would take me under the platform. When the automatic door opened and diverted everyone's attention, I swerved under the platform and crawled far to the back. Squatting down out of sight, I felt good about my rebellion.

I had no plan. My temper got the best of me, but I was right! It wasn't any of these women's fault that someone gave a deadline that couldn't be met! In no one's world should moms have to work until daybreak? I replayed a picture of Mom plopping into bed, too tired to even change into her nightclothes. An irritated voice spoke in my head: *They can try and catch me if they want to, but I'm gonna find a way out and get Officer Matt Darden! He would want to know what was going on in here! I bet he would bring the whole police force in and arrest Miss Barrett!*

I watched for a while and no one was outside. Everyone had gone in and the door was shut. I sat in the dirt, flat on my stomach, looking out to the south when I saw movement across the yard. The bunny! It was following the same trail I had previously ventured on. I went to the southeast corner of the platform and crawled alongside the edge of the mountain, past the automatic door. I would already be in trouble when they found me, so I might as well follow this mountain on around and find a way out! I kept my nose to the ground and moved as quickly as my knees would take me. I came to the corner and rounded it, feeling like I had reached a landmark. I had been here before and knew one more corner for me to be out of sight. I crossed under the classroom windows without stopping to listen. I felt the knees of my pants wearing through. It was too late to worry about that now.

I passed the bunny; he was curious and had stopped to watch me. He was now following me and I was not slowing down for him to keep up. I stopped and rested briefly, then got back on my knees. The bunny passed me, heading to his bushes. I knew when we got to the bushes we would both feel better. I had to stand up and walk the rest of the way; my knees were stinging like fire. The bushes were five or six feet high, and extended twenty or thirty feet in length (depending on whether you counted the bare spots between). I moved back down to the ground to slide into the lower, hollow bottom, and it was a perfect fit. I pulled myself deep enough to feel safe. It felt cool and moist, but not wet. I scanned the length and wondered where the bunny had gone. I closed my eyes to slow my racing heart, and then I felt something cold and wet touch my nose. I jumped, opening my eyes, thinking it was a snake. But it was the bunny who had inquisitively sniffed my nose, most likely wondering why I was in his bushes. He hopped down a few feet and looked back as if he wanted me to follow. I pulled myself with my elbows a few feet and stopped when I heard voices. I remained perfectly still and listened. It was coming from ahead of me. The bunny was sitting on his hind legs looking toward the mountain. Then to my surprise, a hand came from out of nowhere and patted the bunny on the head.

"Hi, baby doll, how are you today?" a woman said. I had never heard this voice and had no way of knowing whether it was friend or foe. So I sat silent. The hand played with the bunny, talking, "Where's your friend today? Have you two been out playing?" I could tell she was a very kind and loving person by the way she interacted with the rabbit, but I couldn't risk everything on that assumption.

The hand finally retreated and I heard a man talking to the women. I listened closely and felt pretty sure it was Sturgis's voice. I ever so slowly pulled myself closer to the window. There were bars spaced only far enough apart for a hand to fit through and only five or six inches tall. No one was on the right side of the room. I slid forward with only a slight push and saw Sturgis sitting on a cot with his arm around a middle aged woman. Her hair was matted, but a faint red tone to her light colored hair told me it could be Mattie's grandma.

It was a small room, with two cots on one wall and a sink and toilet on the other. The door was solid and was shut. I listened while they spoke comforting words to each other. I decided to get Sturgis's attention, let him know I was going for help. I found a pebble and tossed it in. It hit the floor and bounced to the door. Sturgis looked at it, then looked at me. His eyes opened wide and shined with moistness

"I was so hoping you would come back," he whispered as his nose turned red and his eyes watered. I nodded and smiled. "Listen closely," he told me, "follow the mountain on around. It's a long way, but you will come to a stream. That stream goes into the mountain and down to the rollercoaster. You can find a way out from there! You need to get help soon. They are coming to move us sometime tomorrow and I don't think that's gonna be a good thing. He lowered his voice speaking close to the bars, "I heard them talk of getting rid of us."

He moved back and pointed to the woman. "This is Ruth Anne Darden and she discovered what they are up to. Her son's a police officer, and they have no intentions of ever letting her tell him what is going on out here."

"Mattie is okay," I said, looking at Ruth Anne. "She's with my mom."

Ruth Anne closed her eyes and bent her head forward for just a moment; when she lifted her face back up enough for me to see it, the transformation of a relieved look was melding across it. "Thank you so much, I have been worried sick about that girl."

Ruth Anne looked pale and thin. I didn't see any physical trauma on her, but Sturgis had quite a bit of new bruising on his face. He must have put up a fight to distract them from me. I whispered, "Don't you worry. I will make it out and bring back help . . ."

Bang! Bang! Bang!

I fell flat to the ground and could feel the bars encasing the window, shaking from the vibrations. It took me a second to realize what it was. Someone was pounding full force on their closed door.

"What are you two whispering about in there?" a male voice thundered after he banged. Feeling the wetness on the front of my pants, I was sure hoping my pants would dry before I came across anyone.

Chapter Nineteen
Face-To-Face with the Enemy

I LISTENED TO make sure Sturgis and Ruth Anne weren't in immediate danger before I continued on, crawling through the bushes. I could see another small window. I lay quietly to listen; someone was in there. I could hear papers shuffling and an ink pen as it was pressed down scribbling hard and fast. I decided it must be an office worker of some sort. I heard a muffled male's voice talking under his breath, as if he was talking to himself, and then someone walking down a hall said loudly, "Have you got that book-work in order?"

"Just about. They will never know what we been doing. I've got paperwork to back up every transaction. You are a genius, woman. This has been the easiest money I've ever got my hands on. And, sweet baby, half that money is ours."

"I'll believe that when I see it!" I recognized the last voice as Miss Barrett's. "When are they coming to pick those two up?" she asked.

It was quiet for a few seconds, then the male voice spoke, "The last I heard..." He stuttered nervously, then paused.

"What?" she yelled impatiently.

"You need a freakin' helicopter to get down in this place!" he yelled back.

"So what's that mean, Mackle-Bee?" She lowered it a notch and used his name.

"The boss said just get rid of 'em here and bury 'em out back somewhere!"

I laid my head down and closed my burning eyes. Miss Barrett was cursing, then she slammed her fist down onto the table. "I only have one absolute, Mackle-Bee, and this is it," She went from a calm voice to a deep roar, "I don't want any evidence left on this property at all! Mr. Berryhill is coming on Friday, and I want those two gone before then!"

I wanted to memorize the name Mackle-Bee so I could tell the police. But I was so relieved to hear Barrett say they weren't going to kill Sturgis and Ruth Anne here that I took a moment to celebrate to myself. That gave me incentive and maybe some time to get help before they could get a helicopter. Barrett stomped out and I sat waiting. Not a sound was coming from the room. I inched my way forward, not realizing my cargo pants caught on a limb, which cracked and then popped back. I held my breath, praying no one heard it.

"Who's out there?" I saw a big ugly face press up to the bar, so I leaned back as close to the mountain as I could. He reached his arm through the bars and I saw it coming my way! I slid backward, but he grabbed my hair and pulled hard! I screamed and leaped forward with the weight of my body, landing face forward in the bush. He held a huge chunk of my hair in his hand, which included my red ponytail holder. I scrambled out of the bushes and ran. Less than a minute later an alarm went off, it radiated across both sides of the mountain.

"Run, Joey, run!" I mumbled to myself, fighting back the tears. I felt like I was running in slow motion. The rock and boulder infested ground was keeping me off balance. I decided I would try to fool them by climbing the mountain to a safe spot and waiting it out. As far as I knew that big guy was the only male on the premises, aside from Sturgis, and most women wouldn't climb the side of a mountain. The hand that held my clump of ponytail was huge and tattoo-laden. I guessed it was the same behemoth of a man who had dangled Mattie in the air, kicking and screaming. I got a dose of the fear she must have felt. The mountain was huge, so I felt lucky to find a section that had a gradual incline. I had no skills in rock climbing, nor any equipment. I premeditatedly darted back and forth for at least a solid thirty minutes, my goal was to get as far up and away as I could and leave no footprints.

A small grouping of trees that had spastically grown sideways before rising toward the sky caught my attention. I navigated toward them, thinking that would be high enough for a clear view across the whole mountainside. The center tree was nice and bushy, so I climbed into its malformed branches, waiting and watching for at least an hour. No one came looking for me. My reasoning: they were confident I would have to go back around to get out the only door. I sat a little longer, then decided I better move on. I hoped to find a way out before dark.

THE SECRET INSIDE BERRYHILL MOUNTAIN

I moved up high and walked along a rim that seemed to be more fertile. It was lined with small trees and bushes. It looked as if someone had come along with a bag of seeds and spread them in a ten-foot strip around the mountain rim, giving the appearance the mountain was wearing a crown. I stayed above it because it provided a barrier from those below. I was exhausted and focused on a resting spot I saw up ahead—an unusually large shade tree covered in white flowers. I told myself, "You can make it, Joey."

The birds were flocking in and out of the tree and I presumed the flowers had something to do with that. Less than a stone's throw away, the small red fruit amidst the white flowers became visible. The birds worked frantically to carry them away, dropping most when they became too heavy. I picked one up and looked it over. It had the appearance of a cherry, although I had only seen cherries on the top of a banana split sundae. I wiped it off as best I could and took a little bite. My thinking was--the birds would be dead if the berries were poisonous. A little sour, but the juice immediately caused my mouth to crave more. The tree was totally full. I plucked a handful of berries. I rested a while, watching the birds come and go, eating another handful, then pushing as many more as I could in my pockets for later. I was thankful my khaki shirt and pants were loaded with pockets.

The landscape ahead was changing. The trees and bushes were subsiding, and big rocks and boulders looked to be blocking the way. The closer I got, the sound of running water became clear. I saw droplets of water propelling from the rocks. A fresh, dewy rainwater aroma hit my nose. I climbed a tall spindly tree that was close enough to look over and could see a spring trickling down and around several big, flat rocks. It flowed over a long bevy of smaller stones into a stream that disappeared inside of the mountain. Joy filled my heart. *This must be the stream Sturgis told me about.*

Jumping down to go around the large blockade of boulders, I decided I'd better evaluate it first. My choices were to climb farther up—or go back down and around. I chose down. I backed down, hanging onto tree roots and saplings that had managed to grow among the rocks. The dizziness forced me to stop and rest frequently. I sat in the sun on a large, flat deck-like rock that seemed to be sticking out of the mountain. I felt sure I was high enough, I couldn't be spotted from below, but in that same moment, I caught a glimpse of someone out of the corner of my eye. I lunged off the side of the rock to a concave area. I fixated as much as I could, but the sun's reflection affected my vision. I couldn't see anyone coming, and I prayed whomever it was had not seen me. I was so tired and emotionally drained I had to fight for the strength to even consider my options. The berries being squashed in my pockets added to my anguish; it looked as if I had been shot twice in my chest and once in the hip. I had salvaged one pocket. Disengaging from my hidden cubby, I moved upward. After climbing thirty minutes or so, the boulders were getting so large I knew I had the same problem on this side as well. The stream was in the center of massive, larger-than-life unmanageable boulders. I needed to find a way to get to the center.

Chapter Twenty
Waterfall Rendezvous

I EVALUATED THE landscape for a while and decided I needed to go back to the large, flat rock and go up through the center, even though it looked barricaded just above the flat area. The thought of the time lost concerned me, and going back to that wide-open stage of flat rocks would put me in an easily seen position. Navigating rapidly, I passed back and across the sideway jaunt, keeping my eyes roaming for movement. When I reached the rock edge and started back up, I kept my eye on the prize. Pulling myself up and over the flat edge with a forceful thrust from my feet, rolling across the rock, right onto someone's feet. I started to scream and purposed to dive off the side when I recognized the voice.

"Joey, it's me."

I looked up and Mattie, in her khakis and black hair, was sitting on a boulder atop the flat rock. I burst into tears and she did too. "I thought you were that big man!" I told her as I embarrassingly wiped my face. She looked at my red-tinged pockets and was too aghast to speak. "It's just berries." I pulled some out to show her. She sat back down, as that had been a little more than she could handle. "Did you come up from down there?" I pointed down the mountain.

"Yeah," she said. "When the alarms went off, they came to the house looking for you. Your mom was a basket case, so I snuck out to come find you."

I felt my eyes swell. "Is Mom okay?"

"Joey, you know your mom and she worries about you. That's why I came to find you."

"Did you see him?"

"Who?" she asked.

"That giant guy who kidnapped you in the amusement park. He saw me coming this way and I figured he was coming after me."

Her eyes indicated her alarm, and we both scanned the perimeter across and down the mountain. We moved down to the cubby I had found earlier, so we would not be so readily seen. I told her the whole story—how I crawled through the bushes finding the small window. How her grandma put her hand out to pet the rabbit. And what Sturgis had said about looking for the stream that flowed through the mountain, to find the way out to get help. I told her word for word what her grandma said and how she looked.

"Right as I was leaving, someone began beating hard on their door. He didn't come in the room though, and as I was dragging myself away, I came to another window and heard him talking to Miss Barrett, she called him Mackle-Bee and he's her partner in this crime. Your grandma was right, Mattie, they are making the women sew double orders and stealing the extra money!"

This next part might be upsetting to Mattie and I knew

it, but it had to be said. "We gotta find a way out and bring back help, Mattie. Miss Barrett said Sturgis and your grandma are evidence. They are the only two people who knew they were stealing. She wants them gone, that way they can keep it all secret." Now I could see I had pushed her "worry button" and thought I'd better do some damage control. "Sturgis is taking good care of your grandma. He said to get help fast, because he knew of their plans to move them both. That's why I didn't take time to go back and tell Mom. I needed to find a way out and get Officer Darden . . . I mean, your uncle." Her slight nod told me she agreed.

"I have crawled up both sides of these big boulders and couldn't get to the middle of them," I said.

"Why do you need to?" she asked.

"Because. I could hear water running. A stream runs right through the center of all these big boulders, I saw it."

I had made her a believer. She climbed out of the cubby and put her ear to the larger rocks to listen. "I hear it!" she said, scrambling up and over several big rocks until she found a way to infiltrate the center. She pulled me up and the shock and surprise overtook both of us in a monumental way.

"This is incredible," I muttered. The rocks had hidden a small waterfall that was about twenty or so feet inside the crevice. The stream came down from the mountain through the rocks. It entered an opening into the mountain and flowed hundreds of feet down. We crawled onto the ledge that surrounded the pool and into the cave entrance.

"Oh my! Look at that!" Mattie pointed to the massive view inside the mountain; the rails of the rollercoaster could be seen. They were well below this waterfall, but we could see the pattern they tracked circling inside of the mountain. I followed the ledge to the inside and could see another ledge below us.

Mattie shook her head. "No way for us to get down."

We sat down, quite discouraged, to discuss our options. We had an excellent bird's-eye view. I had an idea and plopped down on my belly, scaling across and ending with my head hanging over the edge. Mattie followed my lead. I cupped my hands over my eyes to use as binoculars.

"What are you looking for?" Mattie asked, yelling through the whitewater sounds.

"I want to see if water comes in from somewhere below. Maybe a stream below could be the access Sturgis was talking about."

"I don't see any water but this waterfall. It hits the bottom and flows to the right. How can that be, a stream that starts way up here?"

As I realized this had been nothing more than a dead-end. I spoke to Mattie with discouragement in my voice. "I don't think we can get out from up here." I could tell she had already come to that conclusion and was pulling herself up using the rocks on the side facing as support.

"Joey!" Mattie yelled. "Look!"

I looked to the rock wall where she was pointing. "What is it?"

"This is the same artificial rectangle as the one on the west side of the mountain. It's like a hidden panel."

Mattie was right. Most people wouldn't think anything about this misshapen rock, but it was familiar to those who watched Sturgis open the mechanical door. It was a man-made addition, with a strange brown, oblong shape. She tapped on it. "See, it's not even real rock; it feels like plastic or something artificial."

I tapped it also; she was right, the feel and texture was a little different from the rock that surrounded it. "How does it work?" I asked, then caught myself. "Wait . . ." I jerked my hand up quickly to delay her as I spoke. "They love alarms around here. You don't think it will set an alarm off, do you?"

She shrugged her shoulders and made a nonchalant face. "At this point, what other options do we have?" She was right.

"Okay. Push it, but be ready to run if it sets anything off!"

Mattie nodded and squeezed her eyes shut as she pushed the bottom of the large panel. It popped open and we both jumped back. We had our first hope of getting somewhere! We smiled profusely as we moved back up to look at the now open panel, but still poised to run just in case. It had an intercom screen with a button marked "Talk." It also had a row of five buttons marked, "up, down, open, close and stop."

I moved up closer. "I'm gonna press one," I said, half-asking and half-telling my intentions as I read the buttons out loud.

Mattie held out her hand to stop me. "Let's think a minute." Mattie spoke with a serious voice. "I say we push 'open.'"

I agreed, that made the most sense. "Okay, push it."

Mattie and I took a step back, and she reached out her arm, with outstretched index finger. She pushed. But nothing happened.

"Maybe it's broke," I said.

"Well, if it is, it won't matter if we push some more buttons."

I shrugged and she took that as a go-ahead. She stood back and pushed "close." We heard a motor sound, so we stepped back and watched a wall come down, closing the waterfall behind it.

"That's why nothing happened when we pushed 'open,' because it was already opened," Mattie concluded while we watched it close completely. She opened it back up.

"What do we do now?" I asked.

She stared at the control panel deep in thought. "Let's try 'up' or 'down,'" she alleged with a deep breath.

I nodded. "Okay, do it."

From an arm's length, she positioned herself. "I'm going with 'up.'" She pushed and stepped back. The flat rock we were standing on started to rise very slowly. I looked with panic at Mattie and she pushed "stop." We were standing on a five-foot-wide section that was eight to ten inches higher than the rest of the deck surrounding the pool.

"I don't know about this." I conveyed my reservations, but could see she felt the same by her stance. A piece of Mattie's shirt was clutched between my fingers, and she was bracing herself with my arm. We looked up to see what was above: It had railings on the side facing the rollercoaster and that eased our mind.

"Okay, let's go up," I said.

Mattie pushed the "up" button. We stood close, stabilizing each other as the floor moved up at a slow, but steady pace and then locked into place, connecting it to the metal railing. From this vantage we could see the whole inside, and it was much better than being under the waterfall. The stationary floor extended out past the railing by five extra feet. We admired the construction as we looked out over the Silver Lining Express. It was a work of art how the tracks dipped and curved inside the mountain, utilizing every bit of space. We came to the conclusion that whomever designed and built this was a genius. We ventured back to the other side of the pad, the one we had arrived on, and it had a door.

Mattie peeked through the fogged glass before opening the door. "Wow, look at this." She verbalized her astonishment at a three-sided control panel, which most likely controlled technical support for the acres and acres of amusement rides. Above the control panel, eight monitors had flashing screens displaying various live shots of the park.

"It isn't open yet I guess?" I said, noticing there weren't any people in the screen shots. Mattie pointed to the front parking lot camera, and a line of cars extending at least a mile was moving through a gate being pushed open at that very moment.

"It's almost two," Mattie said. "The park opens at two on Monday through Thursday." We needed to hurry, but at the same time, we needed the park to be full of people to camouflage our being there.

We moved back out front and Mattie turned to me in panic. "I bet whoever turns on the rides will be up here soon!" She had a point.

We looked around to see if there was anywhere to hide. There was nowhere in the control room. We followed out to the railing and spotted a ledge that angled down south from the pad. Mattie found the oval wall controls and lowered the deck. She noticed it had "stop" buttons for one, two, three, or four. One had a waterfall stamped on it. She pushed that one and watched the rock pad lower, stopping at the waterfall. We could hear the waterfall running and felt confident; it was as we'd found it.

As we ventured down, Mattie said in an urgent tone, "We didn't pull the cover back down to blend in with the rocks."

My heart leapt, but it was too late. We heard the floor pad moving. We just had to pray they didn't notice. We scurried down like mice, stopping at the next floor to listen. It was adjacent to the waterfall, but a barrier was blocking it from view.

We could hear teenage boys talking, "Someone forgot to lower the cover on the switch plate."

"Wasn't me—must have been those lazy weekend workers. Not worth the minimum wage they are getting paid."

Mattie and I looked at each other. Did we trust them? There was a chance they weren't in with Miss Barrett and her group. Mattie shook her head and whispered, "We are too close to take that risk." I had to agree.

The sound of the rides one by one being turned on was fantastic. It sent sparks through me. The rollercoaster had lights that systematically lit up and glowed throughout the rail structure, which nudged us to move on down the ledge. Level three had a large pad and we stopped there to let the masses of people fill the park. This section had been added to the mountain and was mostly wood and brown stucco. It bloomed out to the east and allowed the rollercoaster room to flare out and drop down into darkness; it gave the illusion it was descending below ground level. The water was indeed flowing out from the pool we saw it landing in. It flowed along the ground below us and down into a wide crevice that followed closely beside the rollercoaster.

"I bet this is no stream at all," Mattie said, evaluating its progress. "I bet it's a man-made thing to make the ride more exciting."

"Could be, but Sturgis told me a stream ran through."

Some of the lights had gone dim and we worried we wouldn't be able to see, so we ran down the ledge and heard the ride operators talking. Silver Lining Express was moving slowly along the tracks. We were only feet from the track, when I asked, "Do you think the wind velocity from the speed will affect us when it passes?"

"Maybe. Let's get to a better place."

We found an area close to the ground, jumped down, and ran along the ground, hoping the stream would have a shallow spot we could cross. I climbed in the water and Mattie helped me back out, it was too deep to cross and It looked impossible to get out of on the far side; we held hands and ran as we heard the rollercoaster churning into full speed. The sound was thunderous, roaring in and out through the center of the complex. It was coming . . . . Before it overcame us, we fell to the ground and huddled with our arms and legs entwined as close to the wall as we could. I squeezed my fingers in-between two wooden slats and held on with all my might. The centrifugal force pulled for at least thirty seconds as we hung on for dear life. I felt the board coming loose and prayed, "Please dear God help us!" It passed with a sucking force and released us back into the wall with enough vigor that Mattie hit her tooth on the back of my head.

"Are you okay?" she yelled.

Sure, my face hurt from being slammed into the wood,

and I felt a pinhole bleeding in the back of my head, but I yelled, "I'm okay, are you?" She had my hands in hers, and she was shaking, but she nodded her head yes. We knew we couldn't survive another round and had only two choices. One was the water; the other was to break through the wood and see where it would take us. Mattie voted for the latter.

Chapter Twenty-One
Screams of Horror

I FORCED MY fingers in-between two of the loosest boards and pulled. I jerked hard and felt the nails dislodging slightly, but not coming off. Mattie bumped in front of me and used her legs as leverage. I moved beside her, and we both pulled hard and fell back as it snapped off into our hands.

"Can we get through there?" Mattie asked me in a hurried panic because we could hear the rollercoaster coming. I didn't think we could, so I pulled on the next one. It popped out and Mattie scrambled through. I was standing in position to climb through when I saw a huge pair of jean-clad legs. I tried to raise my voice, but it was competing with the roar of the Silver Lining Express. By the time it passed, it was too late—I heard Mattie's muffled screams.

I backed up so he wouldn't see me and fell into the water. The last thing I saw was just like before: Mattie being carried off kicking and screaming. I went under water, swallowing a huge gulp as I sank. When I hit the bottom, I squatted and pushed with my feet as hard as I could to spring myself back to the top. I flailed for something to grab, something to keep me from going back under. I groped along the outside edge for anything. As I was sliding back in, I felt a cable and latched onto it with my finger and thumb to stay above water, then grabbed with both hands, thankful it was stabilizing enough to keep me afloat. Feeling sick, I rested my head for a moment, coughing up a mouthful of water. The ground took on a vibration, and I could hear the coasters rumble. The water sloshed from side to side as I readjusted my grip to ready myself.

The rollercoaster swished by and the panic of it forced my head back underwater. I stayed down and gripped the cable tightly, waiting for the calmness to return, then pulled myself up and took a big swig of air. My head was fuzzy and I had a hard time concentrating on what I should do. Mattie's voice screamed in my head as if she were there. "Run Joey! Run! It won't do any good if we both get captured!" I knew instinctively that was right, I was almost out, I needed to stay focused and bring back help.

I mustered the strength and pulled myself up. The coasters rails now had a full glow of strip lighting, so I needed to stay low and out of sight. I crawled across bundles of cables embedded in muddy trenches. I had no time to worry about the mud. But who knows? Just maybe . . . being covered in mud might be a good disguise.

The walkway with the scenic train murals was in view and several of the ride operators stood on the decking. I ducked and crawled along the shadowed under berth until I realized that I would be seen when the rollercoaster arrived. I backed away from the light, beyond the loading dock into a corner and waited until I had more time. An idea burst into my head and instinctively I knew it would work...if I timed it just right. After this group unloaded and before the new riders climbed aboard, I could jump in the front car and act as if I was the first on to ride. When it unloaded my group, I would leave with the crowd.

I noticed my muddy arms and knew mud had no place in my new plan. I looked for something to clean myself. I found several half-empty bottles of water and washed up the best I could as I waited. The rollercoaster had come to a halt and the ride was being unloaded. I moved close and surveyed the new riders standing behind the chain. I inched my way forward as the chain was lowered. The new riders filled the walkway, making their way to find a seat. Focusing on a moment when the operators' heads were turned, I jumped in the first car, sliding to the far side, hoping and praying no one had noticed. Two people climbed into the second seat.

I only looked ahead but felt the rumble as crowds filled in the seats to the back. Out of the corner of my eye, I saw someone looking at me. I gave the okay, as one determined little boy climbed in the front car with me. That worked out even better than I thought. The well-dressed little boy lowered and tightened our bar, locking it into place. The operator checked it and we were good to go.

I had no idea what a scary ride that front car would provide. We were both screaming so loud the woman behind us patted my shoulder and asked us if we were okay. Before we landed back at the docking ramp, I thought maybe she would be a good cover for me. I had no problem turning on the tears and the boy next to me followed suit. The woman had her arms around both of us as we walked off the loading ramp.

Conformations of joy exploded in my stomach as the sun hit my face. I told the nice lady "Thank you!" As I sped down the Silver Lining's exit ramp. I had made it through the toughest part and ran to a familiar spot. I slid across to the middle of the long bench on the super slide's landing strip, to think. Ravaging through my brain trying to remember where all the cameras were—a whole host of them I needed to avoid. I was starving and so thirsty I was miserable. A strong chlorine flavor from my near drowning had coated and saturated my tongue, making it feel thick and swollen. The trash behind the slide was loaded with half-empty soft drink cups. I found one that still had ice slushing about. I figured if Mattie did that to survive, I could too. I found an almost full bag of peanuts and went back to the benches till I noticed the camera mounted above. I walked to the shade beneath the slide and ate my peanuts, planning the second stage of my escape. I knew it would be a huge risk to trust anyone here. Most of the workers were teenagers, and chances were they would take me to their supervisor, which would put all of us at risk. I looked at every face to see if I recognized any, in a good or bad way. Best-case scenario would be to see Officer Darden, but he was forbidden to pass the entrance gate. That kinda made me mad. Why wasn't he allowed inside the park?

I wondered about Miss Barrett and the giant man called Mackle-Bee. What would they do to Mattie before we could get back and rescue her?

I tried very hard not to think about Mattie. The thought

of it made me feel sick. The idea that these people were prepared to have blood on their hands scared me. I would never forgive myself if I didn't get help before they hurt Mattie or took Sturgis and Ruth Anne away to dispose of them.

To be safe, Mattie's uncle Matt would be the only one I could talk too. I moved to a new spot; I had a feeling I'd better get away from the slide in case that camera caught a good look at me. I worked my way to the southeast, wondering if I could see anything over the ridge and into the backside of the mountain. The Ferris wheel in that area went pretty high, so I got in line. I must have looked pretty bad because I was drawing attention. When I got close to the ticket counter, I found out why. A picture had been taken of me on my entering the compound. The poster tacked to the side of the booth had my face with the word "missing" written under it. I ran. And ran. To the end of that row of rides and behind a building. I sat until dark crouched in a tall patch of weeds, watching the ants crawl in and out of my peanut bag until I finally fell asleep.

Chapter Twenty-Two
Escape Route

I AWOKE AFTER the park was closed. Tossing my ant-filled peanut bag away, I jumped to my feet and frantically scraped all the ants off my arms and chest. I was shivering from both fear and cold, feeling really bad I had let the whole day go by without getting help. I moved as swift and silent as I could, observing closely for anything that moved. I heard trashcans rattling, so I stopped long enough to make sure they had finished their clean-up before darting across the midway. I approached the gate and stepped inside a free-standing vendor's booth. It had a back door that opened to the fence; I unlatched it and peeked through. The tall gate was to my right, and it was chained. My only hope would be if it were loose enough for me to slip through like the gate to the amusement park inside the compound. I made several false starts but stopped abruptly because I was afraid. I gave myself a pep talk, (more like a lecture) whispering, "Joey! You stop it! You big baby! You can do this!"

I forced myself out the back door and pushed the gates apart as far as I could and squeezed. I rearranged the chain and tried again. It was a very tight fit, and it was taking way too long. I darted back to the door to rethink my options. I looked at the gate and chain and decided to try again; this time I wouldn't worry about the chain; I would just use my feet and hands to force the bottom open as far as I could and squeeze through. I grabbed the inside gate with my hands and the outside pushing with my feet. It was working! I put both my legs through and wiggled the rest of my body sideways. I had made it!

I stood up and ran as fast as I could across the parking lot. Having already mapped out a wooded area to the west, I would withdraw into it and make sure no one followed. Making it only halfway, I heard a car start. I turned to look and saw a flash of headlights illuminating across the asphalt parking lot. The high-beam lights were turned on, aimed at me, and lit up my face and body. I froze in fear as I saw the glow of headlights picking up speed across the parking lot, right at me. I got my bearings and bolted, butting across to the closest open grass area.

The sound of the car roared in my ears—it was on my heels and I knew any moment it would overtake me. I hit the grass and rolled as the car slammed on its brakes and slid sideways onto the grass. The rear end landed slightly to the south, but in front of me. I scrambled to get on my feet, then ran in absolute hysteria. My mind was jumbled and I was too panicked to think of which way to go, darting in and out of trees. My legs felt like jelly and were paying no attention to my brain. I was convinced they were going to buckle right under me. Amidst all that was zinging in my head, I realized I heard someone shouting my name.

"Joey!"

The voice sounded familiar, so I slowed and lost my footing as the body behind me slammed. We both slid across the ground through the mud and damp leaves, coming to a stop at the base of a tree. I landed on my stomach feeling as if the wind was knocked out of me. I wiped the mud and leaves from my face and turned over straining to see through the darkness. Only tiny bits of Mattie's face beamed through a covering of her own leaves and mud. But there was no mistaking her thick black streaked red hair, it was distraughtly sticking up and bushed out all over. She was out of breath and speaking, "Why did you run, Joey? Didn't you hear me?"

Ignoring the mud, I pulled Mattie close and hung on, letting out all the emotions I had from the last few minutes of fear. My face was wet and slobbery as I asked how she got there.

"Miss Clarkson . . . She snuck me out after Mackle-Bee put me in a cage!"

I heard the leaves rustling and tried to get up.

"My uncle Matt's here," Mattie said quickly, sensing I was set to run. The view of Officer Matt Darden ducking through the trees brought my tears up again. The headlights from the car glowed against his back, but shined across Mattie and me. I figured my tears were visible and glowing brightly.

Matt stooped beside us and pulled things from my hair speaking, "Are you okay, Joey? Did that tumble hurt either one of you?"

"I'm okay," I said, speaking fast, "but did Mattie tell you? Miss Barrett is gonna get rid of Sturgis and Ruth Anne!"

"Well, I got news for em' it will be over my dead body…" He answered with attitude.

He stood and reached with both his arms to help Mattie and me up. We followed him to the waiting and still running car, which had an occupant.

Matt opened the back door and the dome light came on. A dark figure was sitting in the passenger seat. A woman's voice told Matt to get into the back with me and Mattie, then she slid to the driver's seat. She maneuvered the steering wheel and pushed the gas.

I was speechless not only at the sight of Miss Clarkson in such an in control mode, but also because it seemed we were leaving the parking lot. Something just didn't seem right. My thoughts and fears suggested that I was about to wake up and find out I'm still in the park and this was just a dream.

Focusing on Matt's face, I touched his arm. He was real.

Miss Clarkson looked at me, then glance to the road behind us through the rearview mirror, reminding me of Matts face in the car ride here. She spoke to Matt, "Which way?"

"Take a left and pull in the next dirt road. I'll watch to make sure no one follows us from the complex." Mattie's uncle Matt was breathing heavy. I could sense the stress he was feeling, I figured the imminent danger of his mother, was the cause.

She followed his instructions and went to the east, she made a U-turn on the dirt road, then turned off the headlights. No one had followed.

"Are you sure you don't hurt anywhere Joey?" Matt asked. I shook my head no and he reached his hand and squeezed mine. "I am so proud of you son, very few people have the courage to do what you just did." He looked at Mattie, but still squeezed my hand as he looked back to me. "I shudder at the thought of what could have happen if you and your mom had not been there to help Mattie and my mother."

"How did you get all the way to your uncle Matt?" I asked Mattie.

"Well, Miss Clarkson came and we walked right out the door next to the rollercoaster, no one even noticed. We went to her friend's house and used the phonebook to find my uncle Matt's' number." Her voice picked up speed, flowing with words I could tell she had been holding, "We looked for you, Joey! We hunted as long as we could!"

"Shoot! I wish I would have seen you! That would have saved me a lot of stress!" I said. "They had my face on a poster, stapled to the front of every ride. I ran behind the rides to the tall grass till dark. It never entered my mind you would be looking for me. I had visions of Mackle-Bee hanging you up on a nail!"

"He wasn't so bad this time," Mattie said. "I went without a huge fight, so you could get away." She clicked her tongue, then continued. "I lucked out when Miss Clarkson let me out. Mackle-Bee had goaded me the whole way back, telling me, "Miss Barrett was gonna 'churn my grits' I didn't wanna be there for that."

Chapter Twenty-Three
Backtracking to the Rescue

ONLY HALF WHISPERING, I pointed up to the front seat, "I thought she was one of the bad guys—in on everything." Miss Clarkson looked at me so I worked on a recovery, "I'm sorry, Miss Clarkson, and I shouldn't have said that, I appreciate you helped Mattie escape."

"Until you walk in my shoes don't judge me!" she snapped. Her snippy words drew the attention of all three of us in the backseat. Our heads were turned to look at this scatterbrained, thirty something woman, as she rambled like a mad woman.

"I was—and I admit it. I was one of the bad guys. Believe me, when you get a look at those dollars . . . It changes you. Yea, I sure wanted my cut of that money, but I have morals, I was raised in church. I wanted no part—if it meant disposing of people. But let me tell you something, that gal Barrett . . . she has no problem with being evil! She is almost the devil himself! But she's not the brains though, no, no, no, there's a smart conniver out there somewhere and he's the boss . . . she did hook the group up with an overseas buyer and the secret boss moved her up the ranks . . ."

We listened closely as she ranted, oozing details of the scheme that had taken over the Berryhill home. I don't know if the others noticed, but it seemed to me like she snapped, partway through.

"What made the plan so brilliant?" Miss Clarkson pointed into thin air, "That 'Berryhill home' is a Non-Profit organization, no regulations and no taxes, all profit! It was free and clear money!" She raised her hands voluptuously, in remembrance. "They could make as much money as they wanted as long as it looked like it was going back into the 'Women's home.' She whispered through her funneled hand, "Somewhere the Brains has a stash of over a billion dollars in cash!" She nodded, with a sneaky grin, then tossed her hands up again, this time not voluptuously at all. "Oh well . . . Dynasty's come and Dynasty's go, but they crumble when you get too greedy . . . And old Barrett did. She just couldn't help herself, she had the women making double orders and even adding in clothes made by "others" and saying the Berryhill women made them. For years now she funneled money to someone who was gonna give them their cut, and Briley Barrett was gonna cut me in! It was a great plan till Ruth Anne found out. . . ." She relaxed her shoulders back down and stopped speaking.

We stared at her a full minute after she quit speaking. She glared into the darkness with her hands in her mouth. Matt looked at his watch, while Mattie and I still focused on what we thought had been a quiet, stable, teacher. I had decided she was not stable at all when she chewed the ends of her fingernails off, whispering random words of panic over her monetary loss.

"Who are we waiting for?" I turned my attention to Matt.

"Back-up," he said not even glancing.

"Lights!" Mattie pointed. And way down the road we could see a car creeping our way.

"You kids get out and hide in the bushes just in case it's not a friend." Mattie and I got out and Miss Clarkson followed behind us still speaking to herself.

"What have I done . . . dear lord of mercy, they will find out what I have done . . ." I watched her as she continued walking even after Mattie and I stopped.

"Roger!" Matt patted a big beefy man on his back as he got out of an old truck. "Thank you for coming."

Mattie and I walked back out from the trees to her uncle Matt's car and stood as he filled his friend in on the problem, getting his mother and Sturgis out without anyone getting hurt. It was obvious to me this must be a fellow officer with his short cropped hair, and fully loaded vest, but he wasn't wearing a uniform. He had on green and brown marbled pants and a shirt like a hunter would wear who wanted to blend in with the greenery. His muscles bulged from the almost too small tee-shirt and his boots looked bigger than any I'd ever seen.

Matt walked him over to us and introduced Mattie as his niece and me as "Their best friend." Roger shook my hand.

"That's quite an honor buddy, I thought I was Matt's best friend."

I squeezed my facial muscles to keep from displaying the corny, embarrassed look my sisters laugh at. I slightly squealed as Rogers's firm grip knocked me off balance.

"Where's Miss Clarkson?" Matt asked.

Mattie shrugged her shoulders so I spoke up, "She followed us into the bushes. She was mumbling some crazy stuff about "someone's gonna find out what I've done."

Matt walked to the bushes and yelled her name several times, then came back shaking his head, "We need to get in there and get Mom out before daybreak." Roger agreed.

I feared he was going to leave Mattie and me so I stated our case. "Mattie and I know right where they are! You need in quick! And I know the way in!"

Roger looked at Matt speaking, "I think that's the best way Matt. If we know where they are, we can go straight to them and end this before anyone gets hurt. If we bust in with the whole police force, it gives them time to make sure your momma doesn't talk . . ."

That rang true to Matt, and he ushered Mattie and I ahead of him, "Let's go, and after you show me where Mom's at, I'm putting you both in a safe place!" Mattie and I both agreed.

We trotted at a steady pace and made it to the front gate. Roger pulled a pair of bolt cutters from his backpack and easily snipped the chain from the gate. I eyed it wondering what else he had in the bulging green bag.

I remembered the cameras and told Matt who said we would leave the flashlights off till we got to areas we knew were camera free. The lanterns were glowing brightly in the rollercoaster entrance, "Stay low and crawl to the edge," I said as I took the lead and led them to the easiest place to drop down to the muddy cable filled under world, we had to cross to get to the back of the mountain.

I remembered the stream and stopped in front of Matt, "I forgot . . . there's a really deep stream, I almost drowned when I fell in."

Mattie made sounds of alarm. "Joey . . . ?" She pushed my shoulder. I shrugged.

Roger had already noticed the huge bundles of cables, "Follow the cables, we should be able to cross the water on their backs!" He was right and I kicked myself for not thinking of that when Mattie and I came through.

Past the waterfall we cautiously walked. Roger handed Matt a flashlight from his bag. The illuminating light was helpful, but my stomach quivered from the thought of it being seen by the camera.

Roger was right; a large mound of cables crossed the stream. We strategically crossed one at a time, then worked our way back to the torn off wood panels and crawled through. The flashlights were turned off before we crawled through and my eyes were slow in adjusting. I reached out to grasp whoever was closest and followed along with Rogers backpack clutched between my fingers. He felt me and reached his hand back to grab mine.

The total darkness was smothering and my ears tingled at the newly dominating silence. I listened for any sound, a cricket or owl, anything to break up the empty buzzing my ears were making.

Matt and Mattie had stopped. Roger sat me up on the boulder they were seated at. No one was speaking, we all knew instinctively we were waiting for our eyes to adjust. I looked up and strained to see the sky, but it was void, no stars and no moon, I couldn't even see the clouds that must be blocking them. I heard a faint noise and traced it to my jiggling knees. Gone was the peacefulness of just my stomach quivering, my whole body was shaking as if I was freezing cold. But I wasn't cold.

Matt flipped on his flashlight, "We gotta go and just pray nobody sees the light." Sounds of relief sprang forth. He led the way and we walked at a normal speed for twenty or thirty minutes.

"I'm gonna pick up speed," Matt whispered with a forced unction, "Let me know if I get too fast!"

The sidewalk stopped and we trampled on rocks, as close as we could to the mountains edge, at a fast pace. I figured if Mattie could keep up I could. My legs had gone numb, but I pushed each one forward at its turn.

I recognized where we were. When I stopped to eat berries, I could see this large area of flat rocks lacing the ground below. "We are getting close to halfway!" I shouted to Roger who relayed my words to Matt.

Matt spoke back to me, "Good job, Joey."

After walking and running off and on for a time, I recognized the mountainous terrain as the place I had ran up to escape Mackle-Bee earlier that day, "I think we're almost there!" I whispered loudly, pushing my stiff legs into high gear, so I could catch up with Matt. "Those are the bushes!"

The flashlight was turned off and we walked away from the mountain to the tall grass. Matt wanted to come up with a good plan. "Joey what's the layout behind the bushes."

I cleared my throat of the thick glob that had just settle in. "There are just two windows, the right one is an office and they saw me when I passed by it earlier. The farthest one, the left one is where your mom and Sturgis are. He's her friend, did Mattie tell you?" Mattie's half-smiling face nodded briskly, so I continued, "I tossed a pebble in this morning and Sturgis picked right up on it."

Matt slightly patted my shoulder as he stared at the bushes speaking. "I think I'll let her know were here, before we go around to the front. Maybe Sturgis will have some ideas on how to get in."

He looked apprehensive, with his slow steps, Roger was following, but several feet behind. Mattie and I stood firm till they reached the bushes. We made eye contact, "Let's follow," I whispered. Mattie nodded yes. We followed her uncle, but stayed on the outside of the bushes with Roger. We heard the pebble hit and bounce. Sturgis spoke muffled words and the flashlight came on. The bushes were thin and bare close to the bottom and between each bush. Mattie laid flat to see and I copied. It was obvious, although very discreet, a long over-due reunion was taking place.

Minutes later Matt came out, wiping his wet, red face, recouping from the emotional experience of seeing his mother for the first time in eight years. He walked along the mountains edge, away from the windows and spoke. "Mom's ready to get out of there." He focused on Mattie, "I told her you were with me Mattie. She wants me to leave and get you out of here, but I told her I'm not leaving without her." He looked away, at the triggered emotion.

Roger touched Matt's shoulder firmly, "No chance we are leaving her behind buddy."

"It just rips my heart out seeing her like that, I should have just forced my way back in here years ago because I knew something was wrong!"

Matt kicked the dirt in anger, and Mattie spoke, "I hope you put them in jail forever!"

Matt half laughed, "That's the plan Mattie girl, the long term plan anyway. For right now we need to get you two somewhere safe, so Roger and I can go in and rescue grandma, Sturgis gave me the code."

"We can go to Joey's house," Mattie blurted. "He has a secret room we can hide in!" I knew it sounded suspicious to me, the way she said it, I hoped her uncle didn't see it that way.

"Stay out of sight till we get inside, then find Joey's mom!" he warned, swatting Mattie in passing.

Matt and Roger made it to the corner before I remembered the flood lights, "I need to warn your uncle about the flood lights! I'll run up and tell him!" I ran before Mattie could respond and caught up with them at the corner. Matt was speaking to Roger, "Remember these numbers Roger, '6-6-6-6, Sturgis said that's the door code. I told Matt about the lights and he gave me his flashlight speaking, "Thanks Joey, you guys find a safe place."

Chapter Twenty-Four
Back-Up Plan

"WHAT'S THE PLAN? I know you have one." I spoke a little snippier than I intended. But her eyes revealed she did have a plan.

"Follow me . . ." She turned and I followed her around to the front of the mountain, both of us hugging the wall, to avoid the motioned lights.

We reached the front corner just as Matt and Roger entered the mechanical door. "My plan is to hide under the platform and be ready in case anyone tries to escape!"

We ran across the front and crawled under, watching the door. After 10 minutes I noticed a large pile of something. And in the dark, I imagined it to be a person, although I had not seen it move. I tapped Mattie's shoulder and whispered my fears.

She prepared to turn on the flashlight, "Be ready to run," she whispered, "that's how I always get away!" The quick flash of light on and off revealed a pile of junk with some packing materials.

I released my held breath, relieved it was not a person,

and crawled to the pile while Mattie focused the light on it. I pulled out a thick, long rope and crawled back with it in hand. "We might can use this to tie them up." She puffed her lip and nodded, I guess it sounded plausible to her.

Moments later a rumbling could be heard from the far south sky, we both crawled to the edge, then out onto the open sidewalk to stand. "I wonder if it's the police coming," Mattie said as she looked at the distant helicopter then into my face to see what I thought.

Before I could answer, the stage itself started to rumble and one at a time huge sweeping lights popped on at all four corners. "We need to put them out!" I yelled. "That helicopter is coming to pick up your grandma and Sturgis! I crawled back to the pile I had retrieved the rope from and grabbed two big cement chunks I had seen while I was looking. I handed one to Mattie with instruction, "Bash out the big lights, he won't be able to see to land!"

She knew immediately I was correct in my assessment and ran to the farthest two lights. With one blow to each corner we had them out and were standing in darkness.

We crawled beneath the platform and watched. The helicopter wondered around like he was lost. He searched with a long sweeping light that scanned back and forth across the ground. He was moving our way. I clutched Mattie's hand and my knees were back to jiggling.

"What should we do?" Mattie said, just as an idea popped in my head.

"I have an idea!" I gave her instructions and not a moment too soon, the helicopter landed and was so loud we couldn't hear anything else.

THE SECRET INSIDE BERRYHILL MOUNTAIN

Mattie was in position with a large piece of cement, ready to bang it hard on the metal platform, to imitate trouble close by. I ran to the helicopter just as he open the door. I spoke slow, but with boldness and authority, "Miss Barrett said come back later the Police are here!" I heard Mattie banging the cement on the metal platform several times. He never glanced up, so I thought our plan failed. But moments later police sirens began blaring from the front amusement park!

"See!" I said.

I smiled on the inside as I watched his face for reaction, "Thanks kid! I owe you one!" He started the rotors and lifted straight up.

I was running back to Mattie, proud of our accomplishment, when I heard the mechanical door came to life. It opened and Miss Barrett came running out, waving and screaming hysterically to the helicopter "Wait! Come back!" I hoped and prayed he didn't see her.

The helicopter sound drifted away, but she was still yelling.

"We better hide," I whispered to Mattie.

Mattie had an evil gleam in her eye while we scooted under the platform, she lifted the long rope to show me. I read her mind, but she spoke her thoughts, "Maypole . . ."

"That might work," I whispered.

"You go long and I'll wrap!" She said quickly as she exited from under the platform.

I looped my hand with the rope for a good grip and ran as fast as I could past Miss Barrett who had her back to us.

She saw me dart to her front with my side of the rope, but she didn't see Mattie till it was too late. We ran in circles around her legs till she dropped to the ground, bound tight. She was, so mad she could barely get enough breath for words to come out, "You (blankity, blank, blank) brats! As soon as Mac gets out here he'll put a stop to this (blankity, blank, blank) nonsense!"

The mechanical door was opening, "Run Mattie!" I yelled forcefully. She was already running.

We reached the platform ready to go under, when Roger spoke loud and sarcastic, "Well look out here Matt. Somebody done come along and roped us a big ole Brahma bull!"

Matt laughed, "By golly they sure did," He looked at the two of us, "Kids did you rope that bull?"

Mackle-Bee in handcuffs let out a boisterous laugh as he was placed on the ground beside the bound Miss Barrett.

"Grandma!" Mattie yelled, darting to the mechanical door. Her grandma Ruth Anne stood with several older women, Sturgis was wrapping small blankets around their shoulders. I held my breath to contain myself. I knew these were the women Miss Clarkson spoke of, the six held workers.

I wandered over and waited for the happy reunion to slow down, I didn't want to leave without telling Mattie where I was going. To let Mom know the good news. But Ruth Anne spotted me.

Her eyes were tired and swollen, but she still managed to show a smile. She squatted down in front of me. I looked down when I felt her touch my hands. She had my filthy hands in hers and rubbed them as she spoke, "Son, I can never thank you enough for all you have done. When your sweet little face appeared through those bars and told me your mom was taking care of my Mattie..." Her eyes glassed over with tears. "Well, you gave me hope. I'm ashamed to say I had given up." Sturgis came beside her. She glanced to him then looked back into my face. "You saved my life son, and you saved Sturgis and you saved my granddaughter."

My face grew warm and I looked down to my feet, at her kind words. I had never thought of it that way. I saw Mom and my sister's coming up behind her. But I stayed put as Ruth Anne continued rubbing my hands and speaking.

"Someday . . . Someday, I will find a way to repay you." She shook her head and patted my hands. Mattie came close and laid her head on her eye level Grandma. Her mud stained face was smiling and as usual her bushy, black and red hair was wild and frightful.

When I turned around Mom was there. As soon as I saw her open arms I jumped forward. She squeezed me so tight I could barely breathe. My sisters stood a few feet away and I heard Matt telling them how brave I was to escape and lead him back inside to find his mother. By the time Mom let me loose I was shaking so bad my hands took on a life of their own.

Ruth Anne, Mattie and Sturgis came and stood beside Matt. Ruth Anne quickly wrapped her arms around Mom and rocked back and forth speaking softly, "Thank you, thank you, thank you."

"You raised quite a hero there," Sturgis spoke, patting Mom's back while she was still being held by Ruth Anne.

Mattie grabbed my hand and pulled me away, at the same time a whole squad of police stormed down the dirt stairs from the door we came through on our first day here. We looked up and Miss Clarkson stood waving down from the open Mechanical door. She had obviously been the one to let them in. Mattie and I laughed at her antics as she waved her whole upper body and wiggled her lower body back and forth. Miss Barrett was on her feet now and snarled after seeing Miss Clarkson, "That gal is looney tunes and she needs to be put in a home!"

Sturgis grunted, "I bet Mr. Berryhill will make sure she has a home right here in Berryhill mountain for as long as she wants." I figured Mattie had told them Miss Clarkson rescued her from the cage.

Matt laughed out loud, then nudged Sturgis, "Well the Sergeant just talked to Mr. Berryhill and he said you and little Miss. Ruth are in charge till he can get back here. So I guess that will be your call!"

Mattie was still holding my hand and pulled me back to Mom and the girls, "You guys are still gonna stay here aren't you?" She said to Mom. "The bad guys will all be gone now."

Matt heard her and walked close, looking red and embarrassed. "I apologize Marleen, I had no idea what I was getting you and the kids into."

"Don't you apologize, all things happen for a reason . . ." Mom pinched her mouth to keep from crying as she put her arm around Mattie and pulled her close. "We love this girl." Mattie still had a grip on my hand, so I was pulled close also.

Mattie looked at me with anticipation, then up to Mom, "Does that mean you're staying?"

"Oh yes!" Mom said, joyfully, "We are staying!"

Mom's face was radiant as she laughed out loud, at seeing Mattie drag me along in her happy dance.

Only my sisters and I (and possibly Matt) could see the

transformation that only a few weeks away from Tab had made. The stress she lived under for years by trying to avoid setting his temper off had resulted in her living inside herself—like a shelled, bundle of nerves. The real person she was meant to be--was brightly coming forth.

I sure liked this new self-confident Mom, and the sound of her laughing out loud made my heart tingle. . . .

Author's Note

This book deals with a sensitive subject that doesn't always have a happy ending. I am thankful to my mother, who when I was eight made the same smart decision as Marleen and got us out. We slipped away to a fairytale community and started a new life. If you or someone you know is struggling in an abusive relationship, I have one bit of advice. Tell someone you trust and ask for help. In the same way Matt helped Marleen, my aunt and uncle came to our rescue and set us up in the beautiful community of "Berryhill." Changing our lives forever.

Watch for further adventures of Mattie and Joey coming soon when Mattie comes face to face with her unaware mother and the nucleus of evil is found to be still operating inside the private home.

CPSIA information can be obtained
at www.ICGtesting.com
Printed in the USA
FSOW01n1003291116
27940FS

9 781478 778912